The air rushed against his body, but barely cooled the heat of the demon driving him.

He landed on the ledge of Ramona's building, and imagined her down below, standing before one of her canvases, stroking the brush across the surface. Immediately the erotic paintings she'd completed came to mind, reawakening his desire. A desire only she could satisfy.

He crept toward the skylight and glanced down. There she was, lying in bed, the sheets in disarray around her naked body.

Diego groaned and reared back, knowing how wrong it was and yet drawn to the sight. This was all he could allow himself with her—this distant passion. Anything else was wrong on so many levels.

She was human. He wasn't.

CARIDAD PIÑEIRO

was born in Havana, Cuba, and settled in the New York metropolitan area. She attended Villanova University on a presidential scholarship and graduated magna cum laude. Caridad earned her Juris Doctor from St. John's University and became the first female and Latino partner of Abelman, Frayne & Schwab.

Caridad is a multipublished author whose love of the written word developed when her fifth-grade teacher assigned a project—to write a book that would be placed in a class-lending library. She has been hooked on writing ever since.

Articles featuring Caridad's works have been published in various magazines and newspapers. Caridad has appeared on Fox's *Good Day New York,* New Jersey Network's *Jersey's Talking with Lee Leonard* and WGN-TV's *Adelante Chicago.* Caridad was also one of the Latino authors featured at the first ever Spanish Pavilion at the 2000 Chicago BookExpo America. In 2006 Caridad made an appearance at BookExpo America as one of the authors helping Silhouette launch its new Nocturne line.

Caridad's novels have been nominated for various readers' and reviewers' choice awards, including *Affaire de Coeur,* Harlequin and RIO awards. *Danger Calls* was a 2005 Top 5 Read from *Catalina* magazine and the first book selected for *Catalina*'s cyber book club.

When not writing, Caridad is a mom, wife and attorney. Caridad also teaches workshops on various topics related to writing and heads a writing group at a local bookstore. For more information on Caridad's books, contests and appearances, or to contact Caridad, please visit www.caridad.com.

BLOOD CALLS

CARIDAD PIÑEIRO

Silhouette® Books

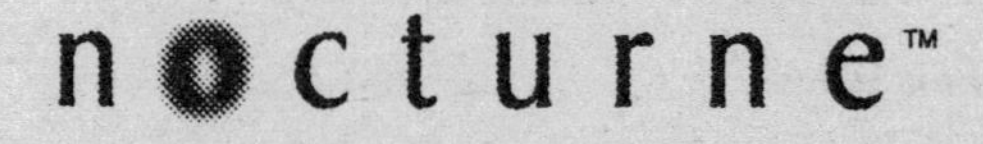

ISBN-13: 978-0-373-61763-0
ISBN-10: 0-373-61763-1

BLOOD CALLS

This edition published by arrangement with Harlequin Books S.A.

Visit Silhouette Books at www.silhouettenocturne.com

Printed in U.S.A.

Dear Reader,

Sometimes I can't believe that we're here, at book six in THE CALLING series. When I wrote the first novel, *Darkness Calls,* everyone told me I would never be able to sell a story with vampires, but Harlequin believed in the story and in me. I am eternally grateful for that since it provided me the opportunity to create this very different cross-genre series that's a little bit suspense, a little bit vamp and a little bit romance.

I've loved seeing the growth of the characters from the first book and allowing you to become involved in the underworld of Manhattan vampires. I hope you're enjoying the continuing mention of characters such as Melissa and Sebastian, and I promise that Maggie and David will soon have their story! I know how popular David has been with so many of you and how sad it may have been to realize that in *Death Calls* David was paralyzed as a result of being injured during the terrorist attack.

I'm working on another three books in the series with yet more of the characters you've come to know—Blake and Stacia for starters, as well as Diana and Ryder again because their story is the foundation of the entire series. Yes, it's true! In a future book, Diana and Ryder will face yet another challenge to their love, one which will propel the series into totally new ground. I hope you'll be back for more! Thanks for all your support and belief in THE CALLING.

Sincerely,

Caridad

To Leslie Wainger who believed in my vampires from the very start and gave me this amazing opportunity to share them with you.

Prologue

1491, Galicia, Spain

The thought of slowly strangling the life from his wife made the flogging almost bearable for Diego Rivera.

As each lash stripped another bit of skin from his back, he imagined his hands encircling her throat. Imagined himself watching her eyes bulge as he exerted pressure and heard the crack of cartilage beneath his fingers.

The pleasure of his near-delirium daydream evaporated as one particularly sadistic blow penetrated his defenses and his body jerked spasmodically.

"Madre de Dios," he gasped as fire erupted between his shoulder blades. Beside the heat of the whip as it tore into his flesh, Diego sensed a warmth that could only be blood trickling down his back.

"Confess your sins, convert. It will go easier if you tell us the truth," the Inquisitor urged from his spot a few feet away. Beside him sat a physician whose job it was to make sure the heretic wasn't too far gone to confess.

This business of saving lives wasn't supposed to kill anyone, Diego thought cynically, then laughed out loud.

The sound bounced off the stone walls of the room, shocking his torturers, who looked at him as if he was crazy. Maybe he was, Diego mused, as he heard the eerie echo of his laughter, sounding too much like that of a madman.

As the physician rose from the chair and walked toward him, Diego realized they would stop the punishment now and wait for him to be more lucid. That was the way it had been for weeks now. Maim, wait, repeat.

It was the way it would be today.

The physician jerked his head toward Diego, and two guards quickly undid the shackles that had been cutting into his wrists. Released from his bondage, he slumped and would have fallen to the ground if not for the guards, who dragged him from the chamber toward the small cell that had held him prisoner for nearly a month now.

They tossed him inside unceremoniously. He landed roughly on the floor, his head smacking against the cobblestones, since his arms were too feeble to break his fall.

What was one more bruise? he thought as the chilly humidity of the cell quickly registered his burning flesh. He shivered violently, which brought renewed pain to his mangled back and sore arms. He tried to quell the chatter of his teeth and swore he would get vengeance on those who had betrayed him.

He didn't know how long a time passed before the slight scuffle of footsteps on the stone floor drew his attention.

"Esperanza?" He glanced upward and smiled as the familiar face of the plain servant girl from his home crept into his vision. Esperanza had been sneaking into the prison to care for him.

"Don Diego, I'm so sorry," she said as she dabbed at his back with a moist cloth.

At his groan, she explained, "This will keep it from getting infected."

Diego knew she meant well, but keeping him alive would only benefit the Inquisitor. He gently laid a hand on her thigh as she knelt beside him. "You are a good girl, Esperanza."

Her gasp confused him. In her vibrant brown eyes, however, he finally saw why she risked her life to help him—she was in love with him. In a way, he cared for her, as well.

Diego had barely noticed her the entire time that she labored in his home. He had been too busy whoring with many more beautiful women, including his own bitch of a wife. His infidelities had been the reason that his wife had lied about him and turned him over to the Inquisitor. Backing her claims that he was a relapsed convert was a lower nobleman who coveted Diego's properties and wife.

God help the poor man when he discovered the real nature of the harridan Diego had married.

A woman nothing like kind and gentle Esperanza, he thought, passing his hand over her cheek. Her skin was soft and smooth and remarkably creamy in color, in sharp contrast to the deep auburn of her hair.

"Do not come again, little one. I am not worth your life," he said, and in truth, he meant it. Selfish and materialistic, he had not been a good man up until now. It had taken this unfortunate encounter with the Inquisitor to make him realize he needed to change.

"Don Diego—"

"Promise me you will stay away." As tears filled her eyes and spilled over, he whispered, "I will never forget you."

She kissed his cheek, then rose and rushed from his cell.

He didn't expect the loneliness that followed her departure. It was a greater torture than any the Inquisitor could visit on him.

Loneliness had been with him for most of his life, he had realized in the weeks of numbing pain and solitary confinement within this small cell.

He vowed that if he survived, he would strive to change that. Strive to do good.

God had to have visited this torture on him for a reason, and he wasn't about to question why he had been called.

He just intended to answer when the time was right.

Chapter 1

2007, New York City

Passion.

It didn't exist in every person who graced the earth, Diego suspected. Only a handful truly knew what it meant to live their lives with such intensity. In the five hundred years since a vampire's kiss had turned him into an immortal, Diego had surrounded himself with artists and others who lived life to the fullest. Who lived life with passion.

Ramona Escobar was such a person, Diego decided as he looked over the latest work she had done.

As he strolled back and forth in front of the six paintings, the vibrant colors called to him, as did the amazing movement and life splashed across the canvases. Beneath it all shimmered the sensuality of the scenes Ramona had depicted in her works—a study of men and women in various stages of making love.

He considered how to best display these paintings in his gallery. He had no doubt he would do so, since they were as wonderful as the others Ramona had done over the years, except…

A yearning existed in these works he hadn't seen before. A need that connected to something deep within him. He had to take a shaky breath to quell the desire that rose in him as he perused one piece. He was sure other people would feel the same and that the paintings would fetch a good price. Possibly an immense price. Thanks to the many centuries he had mingled with the artsy set, he knew how to recognize talent.

"These are wonderful," he said.

Petite and slender, Ramona stood beside him, wiping paint off her hands with a rag.

"Do you think so?" she asked, clearly uncertain. He wondered, as he had more than once during the half-dozen years he'd known her, about the kind of woman she was. One with passion mixed with equal parts humility and doubt. She had matured since the day he had met her, during her final year of art school. He had been intrigued back then by the young, tough ragamuffin with so much talent, but little ego.

But then again, had she been a braggadocio like some other artists he had encountered, he doubted their professional relationship would have lasted this long. Diego did not suffer fools or braggarts. They reminded him too much of how he had been before beginning his eternal life.

Driving that thought from his mind, he said, "Truly unique. They will sell well."

"*Que bueno*. When do you think you can show them?" She continued wiping her hands with the cloth, the gesture telling.

Diego laid his hand over hers. Her fingers were cold, which worried him. "Is something wrong, *amiga?* If it's money—"

"I know you would give it to me. It's nothing, really," Ramona said, and looked up at Diego's remarkable face.

He was so handsome and so honorable. When she had first met him, she had been struck by his elegance and beauty. In the many years they had known each another, he had always done right by her, showing her that his beauty went far beyond his physical attributes. He would do right by her this time, as well.

"I'm fine. Let me know when you want to do the show." She hoped to finish raising the money she needed to care for her mother.

He stroked her hand once again in a gentle

gesture, and, unnerved by his touch, because it made her think of things that weren't possible, she walked away from him. At the table holding her paints and brushes, she set down the cloth.

Diego glanced at the paintings once more before striding toward her. As always, he was impeccably dressed, in a suit that emphasized his broad shoulders and narrow waist. The blue silk brought out the color of his intense ice-blue eyes.

When he stood before her, he tossed his head, sending the longish strands of his artfully highlighted, nutmeg-brown hair back, which emphasized the strong lines of his pale face.

Ramona had always been intrigued by his looks, a product of the Celtic roots in his part of Spain. A Gallego to the core, he would often tease her when she mentioned her own mixed heritage—part *cubana,* part Newyorican and part Irish. The only thing they had in common was a bit of the Celt.

Not to mention that no one had to tell her Diego had known wealth all his life. He had the easy confidence of a man who had never experienced true want.

She on the other hand had known nothing but want since the death of her father, and her mother's illness. And of course, her own illness now.

Ramona was a hard-luck gal, with the hardest luck of all to face—the possibility that she might soon die.

She hadn't said anything to anyone. Not that she

had anyone to say it to, she thought sadly as Diego bent and hugged her. Returning the embrace, she imagined it being more than friendly.

She was shocked when he turned, brushed a kiss across her cheek and whispered, "I'm here if you need me."

At first it had been just business between them, which slowly developed into friendship over the last six or so years. But beneath it all, even from the first, there had been awareness of him as a man—a very attractive man. She had kept her distance, however, knowing of his involvement with Esperanza. But Esperanza had been dead for over a year now.

Ramona reached up and cradled his cheek, brushed her thumb across his lips. Those fine, full lips she had captured forever on the canvas. Had he seen that in the paintings? she wondered. Had he seen that it was him being loved by the stroke of her brush?

"I know, Diego. I'm fine. Really," she replied, but eased out of his embrace. It would be unfair to both of them to head down a road that could bring nothing but pain.

His mouth tightened at her withdrawal, but then he promised to call her later that afternoon about the dates for her show.

"The sooner the better, so I can see *Mami,*" she reminded him.

Her *mami* was too ill to go out alone anymore, which was why Ramona was in a rush to hold the show. Together with the money she had made from creating some copies for millionaire recluse Frederick van Winter, a good exhibit would help her earn enough to hire care for her mother well after Ramona was gone.

She just had to hold on a little longer, she told herself as she walked Diego to the door and let him out of her loft.

She was feeling the weakness that came when she overextended herself. It was time to rest. Soon she would be even too frail to paint, and when that happened…

Without her beloved art, maybe she would be better off dead.

Diego flipped the pages of his calendar, trying to find a slot where he could have a showing of Ramona's paintings.

Fortunately for him, business had been good lately and he had few days available. Unfortunate for Ramona, however. He had gotten the sense that she desperately needed the showing. Maybe money was tight again, he thought, remembering that Ramona's mother had been ill and her care might be a financial drain on the struggling artist.

Although she'd taken advances from him in the past, she had always repaid them from her sales, not that he had asked for repayment.

Centuries of life had made it possible for him to amass quite a fortune. He really had no need of this gallery, but art had always fascinated him. Bored with an eternal existence of doing nothing, he had opened this shop nearly ten years ago after the suicide of a promising young artist he had known. The artist's death had awakened the art world, making him famous posthumously and convincing Diego that he wanted to become a patron of the arts and prevent similar fates for others. He loved the passion and life of the artists. Loved discovering someone who might be the next Velázquez, Goya, Manet or Picasso, all gentlemen he had been lucky enough to meet thanks to his vampire existence.

Then there were the many parties he was able to host when he did a showing. They reminded him of the days before his wife's betrayal, when he'd held such fetes at his estate, many times for an artist whom he had commissioned to do a work for him.

Not to mention that gathering with so many mortals let him make believe for a moment that he was like them. That he was still human.

Human like Ramona, he thought, recalling their embrace earlier that day and the sense of rightness he had felt. The desire that had arisen as he smelled her skin and felt her hair against his face.

All wrong sensations, Diego reminded himself. After his wife's betrayal he had vowed never to let another beautiful face fool him.

Not to mention that Ramona was mortal, and developing any feelings for her would only lead to pain. He couldn't deal with that right now. He had barely recovered from the grief of Esperanza's passing, the woman to whom he had been faithful for five hundred years.

Searching through the schedule once more, he realized there were no openings for at least another two months.

Recalling Ramona's face that morning, he knew she couldn't wait.

He picked up the phone and dialed. As the man answered, he said, "Julio, I've got a favor to ask..."

Ramona couldn't believe her luck. A last-minute problem with another painter had allowed Diego to schedule her showing in a little over a week.

She slept well that night for the first time in months, which left her feeling so refreshed, she decided to give herself a treat. She would go to the auction house for a final viewing of the masterpieces Mr. van Winter was selling off.

She applauded his generosity in donating the funds raised from the sale to the charitable organization his family had founded so many centuries earlier. The van Winter Foundation aided many different causes. In fact, part of her college scholarship had come from a small donation the foundation had made to her art school.

It must have been a difficult decision to donate such amazing works of art. Despite that, Ramona had been slightly troubled by the reclusive millionaire's desire to have copies of the famous works.

She didn't know how he had gotten her name. She only knew that she had been recommended to him as someone with the skills to create worthy imitations of the masterpieces. Despite her misgivings, the money he had offered was more than she could turn down, given her current situation.

She had accepted the job and spent nearly six months painfully and painstakingly recreating the works of the masters.

It had been inspiring to be in the company of such genius. Maybe that was why her latest paintings were so amazing. So filled with passion and yearning.

Or maybe it was something inside of her, calling her to lay her heart on the canvas so that when she passed, someone might know that she had existed. That she had been filled with love, but hadn't found anyone to share it with.

Unless Diego—

Before she let that thought go where it shouldn't, she showered, dressed and headed to the auction house for a last glimpse of the paintings. She didn't regret paying the money to enter the exhibit and see them, only…

Dios mio, this couldn't be right, she thought as she stared at the works on display for the world to see. Three supposed masterpieces, but the longer she stared at them, the more it became obvious that it was her brushstrokes on the canvases. As careful as she had been to recreate those of the masters, an artist always recognized her own work.

Maybe it was a mistake, she thought as she went from painting to painting and carefully examined them for any trace that would tell her they hadn't been done by Ramona Escobar, a mutt of dubious origins with no claim to fame in the art world.

But as she lingered before each painting, scrutinizing every line, loitering over each shadow and color, she realized this was her work being shown. These were her copies and not the originals. And each had been signed with the name of the original artist—something she had not done because of her niggling doubt. In her mind, and possibly that of others, signing them might seem as if she intended to pass them off as the originals.

She hadn't realized how long she had stood there until one of the guards from the auction house came up to her.

"Miss, are you okay? You look a little pale."

Ramona's stomach roiled with anxiety. She placed a hand there to quell its nervous motion.

"Thank you. I'm fine. Just a little overwhelmed by their beauty," she said, and glanced at her watch, finally realizing that she had been there for several hours.

The old man smiled at her and nodded. "They are amazing, aren't they? Mr. van Winter was so kind to donate them to his foundation."

"Yes, very kind," she said, although in her heart she was beginning to question his generosity and intent.

Or maybe she was wrong in being a doubting

Thomas. Maybe the copies were on display to protect the originals. Gazing at the old man and at the other guard at the door, she realized that security measures seemed to be minimal in this area.

That must be the reason, she told herself, but the little voice in her head wouldn't be silenced.

And maybe pigs can fly.

She had no other choice but to attend tomorrow's sale and see for herself which paintings were placed on the auction block.

Diego wanted a last look at the masterpieces. It had been nearly a century since he had seen the Manet.

He had wanted to attend the public exhibition the day before, but Simon, his keeper, had been feeling unwell. Much like Diego, Simon had never really recovered from losing Esperanza, or from the events leading up to her death.

Simon had been caring for Diego and Esperanza, tending to their vampire needs, for nearly a century now, his human life prolonged by the special bite Diego could bestow.

But now the old man said he was tired, and refused to accept the bite that would prolong his life.

Diego understood. Simon wanted to let his life run its natural course. He was ready for what awaited him on the other side.

Diego would honor Simon's unspoken request and the vow he himself had made centuries earlier not to turn another human. After saving Esperanza by turning her, he had dealt with her grief as she witnessed the death of all their loved ones. He had seen her longing every time a mother passed by with a baby in her arms, something Esperanza would never experience.

Her grief and despair had altered her. Although he'd still loved her, he had recognized how needy she had become of him, the one constant in her life. That neediness had made her jealous and petty at times, dependent to the point of almost smothering his love for her.

It had almost kept him from making Simon his keeper, only Simon had begged for life after they had found him in the ruins of his home following the San Francisco earthquake. The keeper's kiss Diego had bestowed had healed some of Simon's injuries and kept him alive to search for his family in the rubble. He had found them a day later—dead beneath the remains of their home.

As Diego had helped Simon bury them, he had seen grief like Esperanza's in the man's eyes. It had only made Diego regret making him a keeper, and had reinforced his decision never to use his vampire's kiss again.

He shook off the unpleasant thoughts, comforted by the fact that he had left Simon ensconced in his favorite chair, watching a History Channel special on the San Francisco earthquake, and muttering about his own survival.

Diego pushed through the door of the auction gallery, but stopped short as he collided with a woman in his haste to see the Manet. He reached out to keep her from falling.

"I'm sorry," he began, but smiled when he recognized Ramona. "I didn't expect you here, little one."

Ramona gazed up at Diego, thinking he looked as elegant and polished as ever. He had grabbed her arms to steady her, and she in turn had placed her hand on the sleeve of his overcoat. The expensive cashmere felt smooth against her fingers, in sharp contrast to the itchy wool of her own peacoat.

She pulled away from him, shoving her hands deep into the pockets of her jacket, both to keep from touching him again and because the chill of the late fall night had bitten into her body.

"I came to see the auction, too," she explained, walking toward a row with two empty chairs. But then she stopped short. "I'm sorry. I just assumed you were here alone, but if you're with—"

"I'm with you," he said with a smile, and confirmed her choice of seating.

Ramona told herself he was just being kind, much as he always was, but it was tough not to imagine how it might be if it were different. If he saw her not as an eccentric, reclusive painter always living on the edge, but as an attractive woman.

Although how could he? she wondered, gazing down at the coat that was a bit too big on her, thanks to all the weight she had recently lost. Even before her illness, his actions had been nothing other than brotherly. She'd always admired his faithfulness to the woman in his life.

When she sat, he paused to remove his overcoat, and revealed yet another fine silk suit and shirt. The top two buttons of the shirt were open, exposing the curly, light brown hairs on his chest. She wondered whether that hair would be crisp beneath her fingers.

"Ramona?" Diego said, and she realized that he had asked her a question.

"I'm sorry. What did you say?"

"Do you want to take your coat off?"

Cold lingered in her body from the autumn night, so she shook her head. "Not just yet."

He sat beside her, his size and strength striking her again, but she had little time to think about him as the auctioneer came to the podium.

She leaned forward, eagerly watching as a covered painting was brought in and placed on the easel. A hush fell over the room, replaced by murmurs when the painting was unveiled and the auctioneer named the opening price. Fifteen million dollars.

She held her breath, examining the painting from afar. She told herself it must be the original, but once again her artist's eye could pick out the differences. Why hadn't anyone at the auction house seen that this wasn't the authentic masterpiece? Why didn't any of the prospective buyers realize it?

As the bidding for the painting climbed ever higher, she shifted closer and closer to the edge of the chair, her arms wrapped tight around her to ward off the frost filling her body. When the bidding ended at thirty million, she gasped, shocked by both the price and the fact that it seemed as if van Winter was going to get away with his deception.

Diego's hand lit on her back, and she glanced over her shoulder and met his concerned gaze.

"Estas bien?" he asked, rubbing his hand against her shoulder in a soothing gesture.

"I'm fine. I just can't imagine…" She wanted to say that she couldn't believe that no one had realized the fraud, not even Diego, who was usually so astute.

"It is a lot, but one day you may command similar prices."

"Sure. When I'm dead," she muttered, and Diego chuckled, not realizing the irony behind her statement.

"Do not worry, little one. Your day will come."

She forced a smile and fixed her attention back up at the front of the room. As had happened for the first painting, the next two were sold swiftly.

All three of *her* paintings fetched a grand total of nearly one hundred and twenty million dollars.

She wanted to stand up and shout to everyone that they had been deceived, but who would believe her?

This was one of the city's better known auction houses, selling off paintings for one of the world's richest men, and she was no one.

Merely the struggling unknown who had unwittingly helped him carry out the deception.

A sick feeling twisted her gut, and the chill that hadn't left her all night made her numb inside, weak, she realized as she tried to stand, and found that her legs were a little wobbly. The anxiety and the late hour had taken their toll on her.

"Ramona?" Diego questioned, but she couldn't answer as spots began to dance before her eyes.

She had pushed herself way too much, she realized as Diego slipped his arm around her waist, providing stability.

"Let me get you home," he said, and she didn't argue, lacking the strength to make the trip on her own.

Besides, she needed to conserve her strength for what would be a tough road ahead—proving that van Winter had sold forgeries, and even more importantly, clearing her name of any involvement in the crime.

Chapter 2

So maybe he was wrong to be taking advantage of the fact that she was feeling unwell, Diego thought. But it was the first opportunity to be close to her since Esperanza's death. He had noticed Ramona well before that, but being an honorable man, unlike he had been in his human life, he had banked his attraction to her.

Even now a part of him said this wasn't right. She was human and he was undead. He could offer nothing, but he couldn't deny that he liked the weight of her in his arms as he held her on his lap the entire cab ride home.

She murmured a protest when they arrived at her loft and he insisted on carrying her upstairs. With his vampire powers, he barely registered her weight. Actually, even with just his human strength he could have easily managed. She was so petite. Thinner than she had been a few months ago, he belatedly realized.

It brought out protective feelings in him that should have sent up major warning bells. The last woman he had felt this way toward was Esperanza, and look how that had ended. With death both times.

But that didn't stop him from depositing Ramona on the sofa in the living area of the large loft, and getting her settled. Despite her continued reassurances that she was fine, he insisted she rest while he prepared some tea, since he noticed yet again that her hands were ice cold.

Way too cold, combined with way too pale…

Diego opened up his vampire senses, but found Ramona's energy to be totally human and a little frail. The hunter in him recognized she was easy prey, but he tamped down such a thought.

He hadn't fed from an unwilling human for quite some time. He wasn't about to begin now.

Although the look that she gave him as he approached with the tea hinted that Ramona might not be so unwilling.

Handing her the mug with the honey-laced concoction, he sat on the coffee table before her.

"*Gracias,* Diego. You didn't have to do this." She cradled the cup with her long fingers, her actions graceful as she brought it to her full lips and took a delicate sip.

Desire rose in him again, much as it had the other day. Intent on fighting it, he said, "I need to take care of my investment, don't I?"

A crushed look swept across her features before she contained her emotions. "Of course. I understand how expensive it is for you to show—"

"Your masterpieces," he said, and because he couldn't sit there any longer, staring at her wounded, doe-brown eyes, he rose and stalked across the loft to her work area.

As he had two days earlier, he stood before her paintings, admiring the sweep of her brush as it almost made love to the figures she had placed on the canvas. The movement of the brushstrokes was so alive, he found himself laying his fingertips against the image on the canvas as if to prove to himself that they weren't real.

Ramona wondered what he was doing as he stood there, scrutinizing her artwork once more. When he raised his hand and touched the canvas, she had to go see what had drawn him. She set the mug on the table and joined him.

When he ran his fingertips along the line of the woman's hip in the painting, tracing the slender sweep of her waist, Ramona imagined his hand against her own body. Imagined how it would be for him to touch her the way he caressed the woman on the canvas—the woman she had imagined herself to be, lost in the throes of a lover's embrace.

As he shifted his hand upward, over the shadow beneath the woman's breast, she felt his energy beside her. Sensed his growing desire and her own.

When he looked at her, his ice-blue eyes blazed with fire. "Did you feel this way as you painted?"

She had felt that way and more. But she couldn't confess that with each stroke of the brush, she had imagined it was them together.

"No," she said.

But he faced her and, laying a hand at her waist, murmured "Liar."

He bent from his larger height, but she was already meeting him halfway, wanting to experience him if only for this one moment. A moment that had sprung from nowhere, but was not to be missed.

His lips were a bit cold, but wonderfully soft on hers. They sampled the edges of her mouth as he wrapped his arms around her, pulling her close.

The body she had admired from afar was much like she had imagined. Big. Strong. Firm.

He was hard beneath her hands as she grabbed hold of his shoulders. Hard against the flatness of her belly as he swept his arm beneath her buttocks and drew her to him.

She moaned at the thought of that hardness within her. Of his big body urging her downward into the softness of the bed that was just at the other side of the loft.

Her whimper of need jolted Diego from the enjoyment of her response.

As right as she felt in his arms, this was wrong, he thought, and slowly eased away from her.

"*Perdóname,* Ramona. This should never have happened."

"You're right. I'm sorry, too," she said, and shifted away, nervously rubbing her palms up and down the front of the figure-hugging jeans she wore.

He reached out and took her hands to stop the jittery motion. "Please don't take this wrong, little one. It's not you, it's me."

"You're gay?" she squeaked, obviously confused by his statement.

"No, not at all," he began with a chuckle. "I'm just a...heartbreaker. A cad."

"A cad? Fossilized much?" she teased uneasily at his choice of the rather old-fashioned term.

"Let's just say I'll break your heart, and I'd rather not do that."

She slipped her hands from his and nodded. "I get it, Diego. No harm, no foul."

"Right," he said, only he didn't think either of them believed that there had been no harm.

After the heat of that kiss, their relationship would never be the same, and that wasn't a good thing.

Diego was always amused by a visit to the Lair. His friend Ryder had managed to create quite a tongue-in-cheek homage to his vampire self. From the faux stone walls to the hundreds of realistic bats clinging to the ceiling, everything about the establishment created the illusion of being in a cavern deep belowground.

As Diego strolled to the bar, he smiled at the sign for the club, which dripped neon blood from its bright red letters onto the gleaming stainless steel surface below.

Diego realized the crowd here only liked to play at being in the darkness, unlike those who frequented the Blood Bank, where he used to hang out before meeting Ryder nearly two years ago. Up until then, he and Esperanza had visited the place fairly regularly, knowing that they could always sip from a willing neck or drink the bloody libations the Blood Bank carried for its vamp clientele. Totally unlike Ryder's club, which had a strict No Bite No Blood policy.

Diego had to acknowledge that coming here and being with Ryder had mellowed him somewhat, making him more of a human wanna-be than ever before. Maybe that was the reason Ramona was now so intriguing. Hanging with Ryder and his friends the past two years had blurred the lines between his true vamp world and the human world to which he could never belong.

Or maybe it was because his friend Ryder was in love with a human—something Diego refused to consider.

Ryder approached, his mortal lover at his side. Diana didn't look well, Diego thought; her pale countenance and slight frame seemed even more delicate than it had just a few weeks ago, when he'd last seen her. As she neared, his vamp senses picked up the unusual thrum of power cast from her body, and he shot a puzzled look at Ryder.

Had he turned her? he wondered, sensing that there was something more vamp than human about Ryder's lover. However, Diego knew if there was anyone more adamant than he about not turning anyone, it was Ryder.

"How are you?" Diego said as he rose and embraced Diana, sensing the fragility in her petite body.

"I'm fine. What brings you here?" she asked, slipping onto a stool beside him.

Ryder took a spot behind her, clearly offering her support. She shot him a look that was both grateful and sensual, as if just his touch could rouse her.

Diego realized it was enough for his friend as he bent and nuzzled the side of Diana's face in a loving gesture, a human gesture. Even when Ryder dropped his head lower, to the crook of her neck, the vampire stayed in check.

With the scene too painful to behold, Diego turned away, focusing on the deep red of the wine in his glass. He imagined it was a fresh O positive, to remind himself of what he was. Of why emotion such as that plainly visible on Ryder's face would bring only pain and despair.

As Diana picked up her own glass of wine, he once again wondered at her paleness and the power spilling off her body. Of course, Ryder was plastered so close that maybe it was a remnant of his vampire energy that Diego sensed.

But maybe it was time to press the issue.

"Bite any good necks lately?" His gaze skimmed to Diana's jugular before he took an idle sip of his wine.

Ryder straightened, an angry look on his face. Diana flinched at the remark and her own face darkened with anger.

"Something on your mind, Diego?" Ryder asked, easing his hand to her shoulder, where he rubbed it back and forth as if to soothe the prickly special agent, who was clearly not amused by Diego's comment.

"Diana just seems a bit…under the weather. Maybe she needs a more experienced vamp—"

The human Ryder had been the one to escort Diana to the bar, but it was his demon side now acting with a vehemence and swiftness Diego hadn't expected. He found himself lifted off the stool as Ryder snared his neck in one strong hand.

"Why are you doing this?" his friend hissed against his face, his eyes bleeding out to an intense blue-green as a hint of fang slid downward.

"Woman trouble," Diego confessed. For the last

hour he had prowled Ryder's vamp-themed club and engaged in dances with an assortment of nubile young women in the hopes of driving Ramona from his mind. When he realized that every female he had chosen reminded him of the eccentric artist, he'd given up and decided to resort to wine to force thoughts of her away.

Diana laid a hand on Ryder's arm, urging him to release Diego, which he did. She slipped from her stool and said, "I'll let you two talk. Be back later."

With a quick kiss on Ryder's cheek, she walked away, leaving the vampires alone. Reining in the anger that had brought forth the demon, Ryder said, "It's been over a year now. Don't you think it's time you forgot about Esperanza?"

"You can never forget a true love, but actually, this is about someone else."

"Someone else? This warrants something stronger than wine, I believe." Ryder motioned to a waiter. "A bottle of Cuervo and glasses, please."

The bartender obliged. He placed a shaker of salt and a small bowl of limes next to the tequila.

Ryder poured full shots of the liquor, then grabbed his glass. Heedless of the salt and lime, he held it up and said, "To women."

Diego shook his head. "Never again, *amigo*."

"But you said—"

"Woman *trouble*. As in major mistake never going to happen in my eternal life if I can help it."

With that said, he slugged back a full shot. He quickly refilled the glass, prompting a chuckle from his friend.

"This is serious. I've never known you to have more than one."

With a careless shrug, Diego took his time with the second drink, sipping the tequila slowly. He winced at the sharp taste of it, so much less pleasing than either a glass of wine or a nice nip from the neck of someone willing.

Like that attractive young woman eyeing him from the end of the bar. She was barely thirty, with long chestnut-colored hair and dark eyes much like—

No. He hated that his thoughts had strayed back to Ramona. After Esperanza's death, he had assumed he would spend the rest of his eternal life sans partner. That Ramona kept intruding into his psyche troubled him deeply.

"So tell me, Diego. Who's the unlucky vamp who's displeased you so?"

In the vampire hierarchy in Manhattan, Diego's age and corresponding power put him high on the pecking order. Those who angered him could be handled without encountering much opposition from the other vampires in the city. Not that Diego took advantage of such rank. If anything, the other vampires considered him a human wannabe because he normally refused to benefit from his powers and his undead state.

As for Ramona, she knew nothing of his eternal life. Nothing other than the face he presented to the mortal world—that he was a well-off dilettante who had rather successfully dabbled in the art world. He imagined that like most humans, Ramona would not be able to deal with his true self.

"Diego?" Ryder prompted at his delay in answering.

"She's not a vampire. She's a mortal."

Ryder shook his head as if to clear it. "Did I hear you right? A mortal? Like Diana?"

Diego thought about Ryder's mortal lover, only Ramona was nothing like Diana. With a shake of his head, he teased, "*Amigo,* there isn't anyone quite like your lover."

Ryder looked toward Diana, who was busy talking to someone at the edge of the bar. He tarried in refilling the shot glass before bolting back another slug of tequila.

"Is everything okay with you?" Diego asked, sensing his friend's suddenly troubled state.

With a shrug, Ryder said, "Diana has been tired lately."

Diego sensed that it went beyond tiredness, but if that was what his friend wished to call it, he wouldn't worry him more. "I'm sure she's been working long hours on some case."

"I guess desk duty can be difficult."

Desk duty would be the death of someone like

Ryder's very empowered lover, he thought. "They still haven't released her?"

"No. The review board suspension hasn't been lifted. But enough of that. Who is this mortal woman who has you so twisted up?" Ryder asked, starting to refill their glasses for a third time. Diego waved him off. "I'm afraid I may need something more satisfying, *mi amigo.*" Something that would remind him of what he was and why someone like Ramona Escobar was thoroughly wrong for him.

"I'd go with you, but…"

Surprised, Diego shot a puzzled glance at his friend. Ryder only occasionally indulged his vampire needs, usually at times of extreme stress, when releasing the beast within helped restore balance.

It also helped restore the reality of their situation—that they were no longer human. That playing at being so and acquiring human desires and attachments could only bring eternal pain.

Slipping from the stool, Diego clapped his friend on the back. "*Comprendo, amigo.* However, a willing neck waits for me at the Blood Bank."

Chapter 3

Diego slipped payment to the vampire guarding the back rooms and walked past him with the young girl in tow. She was medium height, with short red hair and a plain face, but her body made up for it. The black leather she wore exposed womanly curves and alabaster skin. She was much like Esperanza, who beneath her servant's clothes had been blessed with a voluptuousness that he'd lovingly cherished for five hundred years.

He opened the door to the first room, one of a series that Foley, the owner of the Blood Bank, kept for those who wanted some unusual enjoyment. As Diego entered, he noted the chains, whips and other accoutrements on the far wall.

When the young woman saw them, she let out a squeal of delight and rushed over, selecting a small whip, which she snapped with relish.

The noise unnerved him, and in a blast of vamp speed, he raced forward and ripped the whip from her grasp.

She glanced up at his face, her head tilted at what she probably thought was an engaging angle, but which only served to expose the pale skin of her neck and the pulse that beat there.

"What's the matter? Afraid of a little pain?" she asked coyly.

Diego laid a finger on that pulse point and met her gaze. "You know nothing of real pain," he said, his tone soft but threatening.

"Really? But I know one thing." She leaned closer and reached down to stroke him through the fabric of his pants.

"Yes, you do know." He sucked in a breath as she undid the zipper, slipped her hand inside and beneath his briefs to wrap her soft palm around his rock-hard erection.

"You like?" she asked, and at his nod, she dropped to her knees, freed him from his pants and took him into her mouth.

Dios, Diego thought, enjoying how she satisfied him with her gifted mouth and tongue, while wondering at the same time why modern women debased themselves so quickly in this fashion. In his day, only the street whores would go at a man like this, without prelude or passion.

But that thought didn't stop him from holding her head to him until he felt his climax rise to the edge, and with it, the beast who needed satisfaction of another kind.

Shaking his head, he drove the demon back, wishing to at least pleasure the woman before he allowed his own release and indulged the vampire with a different kind of fulfillment.

Urging her to her feet, he undressed her slowly, revealing each luscious curve. He paused to caress her generous breasts, which filled his hands, and the large, rosy peaks of her nipples. She moaned as he sucked at them, but with a little love bite, he moved lower down her body until he was the supplicant before her, peeling away her leather pants to reveal the nest of auburn curls between her thighs.

She gazed down at him then, her brown eyes dilated with passion, her lips full, not that he would kiss her. He never kissed any of his conquests on the mouth.

Instead he grasped her hips and urged her forward. He nuzzled the curls with his nose and then slipped his hand around and parted her, eased one finger and then another into her while he licked the nub between her legs.

She gasped in delight and grabbed hold of his shoulders. Her soft moans drove him on, until he could wait no longer. Surging to his feet, he raised her off the floor and drove into her before walking them to the far wall of the room.

With her back against the rough plaster, she shifted her hips, moving on him, and he hammered into her again and again until she nearly screamed from the force of his thrusts and the pleasure they wrought in her.

The pulse at her neck beat rapidly. Violently. Blood called him to fulfill another need.

Diego bent his head and placed his lips there. He licked her skin, finding it slightly salty from the sweat of their lovemaking. Sweet beneath the sweat.

She shot him a look from the corner of her eye, and he whispered against the side of her face, "You know what I want."

At her nod, he surged upward into her one last time, liberating a climax that made her scream.

Then he finally freed the demon. His eyes bled out and fangs erupted from his mouth. Fangs that he drove deep into the skin at her neck.

Her body tightened around him, held him closer as the vampire's kiss created a different kind of hunger within her. Within him.

He sucked, savoring her blood, singing with the passion from their sex. He felt filled with youthful energy. Her blood charged every inch of his vampire body with renewed strength.

He could have kept on feeding, as many did,

until there was no choice but to turn the human or let her die. Instead, he took only enough to sate the night's hunger, knowing that tomorrow there would be another willing human or a delicious libation at the Blood Bank.

Rearing back, he carried the nearly unconscious young woman to the bed. His hands trembled with the energy zipping through his veins from his feeding, but somehow he managed to rearrange her clothing and his.

As he gazed down at her, she seemed to be peacefully asleep. The bite marks on her neck were already healing. When she woke, she would feel as if she merely had a bad hangover, and remember little of their encounter.

And what will you feel when you wake? the voice inside his head asked. But Diego knew there was no waking from this eternal nightmare. From the endless days filled with only one certain thing. Death. No end to the loneliness that had returned with Esperanza's death. Especially not with a human, he reminded himself. With a last look at the woman, he fled the Blood Bank. Though hunger was abated, the encounter had left him unsatisfied. He dived into the night to find a different kind of delight.

With the energy of the young woman's blood rushing through his veins, Diego leaped up to the rooftop of the adjacent building. A harvest moon filled the night sky, illuminating the city below, lighting the night for him, as if knowing of his intent.

A burst of vamp speed had him nearly flying over the rooftops, vaulting from one building to another in his haste to reach his destination. The air rushed against his body, but barely cooled the heat of the demon driving him. With one last, almost desperate jump, he was on the ledge of Ramona's building, an old converted warehouse in a part of town that had yet to be gentrified. It was probably why she could afford to have the uppermost loft. It boasted skylights at various locations that flooded the space with light so she could paint.

He imagined her down below, standing before one of her canvases, as he neared one skylight. Imagined her stroking the brush across the surface, and immediately the paintings she had completed came to mind, reawakening his earlier desire. A desire that taking the young woman hadn't satisfied.

He suspected only one woman could slake his need tonight.

Slowly he crept to the skylight and glanced downward. The paintings were there, but that wasn't what he wanted to see.

He shifted to the next skylight—smaller than the first, but still generous enough to provide a view.

She was there, below the glass, lying in bed, the sheets in disarray around her naked body.

Diego groaned and reared back from the sight, knowing how wrong it was, and yet unable to deny himself this. This was all he could allow himself with her—this distant passion. Anything else would be wrong on so many levels.

She was human.

He wasn't.

She would die.

He wouldn't.

He couldn't keep her with him. He wouldn't turn her and see her change. See all that he admired about her become twisted by the grief that would inevitably follow as the years passed and life went on around them. As loved ones and familiar things were lost.

He had seen how it had affected Esperanza. How it had touched the lives of Ryder and all his other friends. He had encountered one too many vampires whose hearts had grown cold, or who had gone nearly insane from the loss of those for whom they cared, and all they held dear.

He wouldn't visit that kind of distress on anyone else. But he wouldn't deny himself satisfaction this night, he decided, as he inched back to the edge of the glass and peered down.

Her breasts were full and as beautiful as he had imagined, with dark coral nipples he hungered to taste. The sheet draped across her body just beneath her breasts, the dark maroon color highlighting the paleness of her skin and accenting the chestnut highlights in her hair.

She shifted in bed and her long dark hair fell against her breast. She brushed the errant lock away, but then paused, her hand lingering there.

Diego swallowed back a groan as she touched herself, cupping her breast and fingering her nipple until it peaked to a hard point.

She was awake.

With his vamp senses he could detect the rhythm of her heartbeat and breathing, which said she was conscious of what she was doing. He could hear the beat grow faster and see the pulse in her neck jump as she played with the tip, rotating it between thumb and forefinger. Pulling and pinching it as a lover might.

After their brief interlude earlier that night, was she imagining that it was him?

At the thought, his erection swelled painfully against his jeans, human desire overriding the demon. As wrong as he knew it was, he couldn't pull away from the sight of her, couldn't stop himself from reaching down and imagining it was her palm on him.

His mouth watered as she moved her other hand downward, past the rounded curve of her hip visible above the sheet. He stroked harder as her fingers found her center beneath the sheets, and the beat of her heart surged in response.

When her hips raised off the bed, he groaned and closed his eyes, imagining how he might grasp those hips and drive into her. How he might stroke her to a release the way he now pulled at himself, harder and faster as his vamp senses picked up the erratic breaths spilling from her lips. He heard the soft moan of desire followed by a sharp gasp as fulfillment chased through her body.

He came then, violently and so swiftly he grew light-headed from the force of it.

Dropping away from the skylight, he sat at the edge, spent. Humiliated at how little control he had exhibited. Only it had been so long since he had felt such need. And it wasn't just since Esperanza's death nearly eighteen months earlier. Diego realized that it had been too long since life and passion had filled his being. Since he had truly lived.

At that, he bent his legs and buried his head in his knees, tears threatening as he realized the emptiness of his life. Of all that had been his existence for five hundred years.

Just because one woman's passion had roused him as never before. A woman he could never have.

With a rough breath, he forced himself to rise and put things to right, but as he did so, he allowed himself one quick look before he left.

One look too much, he realized, when he saw that she had curled up into a ball and was crying. Her tears tugged at his heart, but before he did something he would truly regret, Diego surged off the roof, the sight of her crying driving him away, since all he could do was bring her yet more tears.

* * *

Ramona dashed the tears from her face, chastising herself for her weakness. She should never have given in to the remnants of the dream—one filled with her and Diego making love.

But she had let her need guide her, and the physical satisfaction she had given herself had been gratifying at first. Then the realization had come of how empty it was. Much like her life. Much the way her life would end.

Empty and alone.

She had spent her early teen years struggling to survive in the barrio, joining a small street gang for protection and company. With her dad gone and her mother slowly losing her mind, there hadn't been anyone else to turn to.

A bad mistake. Their petty thievery and rivalry with another gang had landed Ramona in juvie for a few difficult months. It wasn't the time in the detention center that had been hard, it was worrying whether her mother was coping alone. Luckily, a caring counselor had helped her out and provided her mother with a visiting nurse.

That and an art class during her incarceration had set Ramona on the path to a college scholarship. After, she had devoted much of her later teen years and early twenties to her art, perfecting it at the cost of a social life. Any time not in the studio was spent caring for her mother at home, until the Alzheimer's worsened and her mom had to be institutionalized.

Ramona had dated now and again during the last few years, but had found no man she could imagine spending the rest of her life with. No man as attractive as Diego, who had become her patron shortly after her graduation from college.

Now thirty was just a stone's throw away, only she wasn't sure she would reach that age. She had been battling the anemia robbing her of life for almost three years, since the diagnosis that had rocked her world.

Dying didn't bother her as much as the thought of dying alone and unsatisfied. Of dying without ever knowing the kind of love she had seen her parents share before her father's own untimely death and her mother's illness.

Diego, she knew, was capable of a love like that. She had known of his devotion to Esperanza and had seen his pain after his lover had passed.

What would it be like to love or be loved like that?

Sadness filled Ramona as she realized she could never explore her attraction to Diego. It wouldn't be fair to him, because of her illness. Not to mention that they were from such different worlds, his one of wealth and hers of the streets.

Had she stayed in the old neighborhood, stealing would have been part of her life. A life possibly meant to end quickly by gang violence.

Her art had helped her escape the streets, but not her fate—a life cut short, and tainted now by the fact that her skills had helped someone steal from others.

She should have realized something had been odd about van Winter's request and refused it, but she had been desperate for the money for her mother's care.

But maybe Ramona hadn't been deceived. Maybe there was some rational explanation for why her paintings had been on display.

As she settled back against the pillows, she knew she had to find out and make things right.

Her stint in juvie had hurt her mother and dishonored her father's name. She didn't plan to die with people thinking that she was thief.

The facility Ramona had chosen for her mother supposedly provided the best care for patients with Alzheimer's disease. But what had cinched the selection had been the wonderfully manicured grounds and almost parklike settings around the buildings.

Her mom loved the outdoors, and Ramona knew the lush gardens and lawns would give her joy even when she could no longer understand anything else.

It was the reason Ramona didn't mind the long ride out on the railroad to the institution, although she regretted that her own illness had cut back on her visits. Lately there were days when she didn't even have the strength to get out of bed, much less spend several hours on the train. Beyond the physical demands was also the emotional drain of seeing her once loving and caring mother fade before her eyes. It was sometimes more than Ramona could bear.

She had been feeling physically stronger today and needed to visit, to talk with her *mami* about all that had happened. If it was a good day, her mother might actually be able to understand bits and pieces, and listen and nod. Ramona imagined those nods to be answers and not just twitches.

On a bad day, her mom would stare at her vacantly, as if she didn't even know she was there, much less recognize her.

As the train chugged along, making stop after stop, Ramona prayed today would be a good day.

She arrived at the facility nearly two hours later, and was greeted by the receptionist.

"Ms. Escobar. So good to see you again. Dr. Cavanaugh wanted to speak with you if you have a moment," the woman said as she handed Ramona a visitor's badge.

"Of course, Mabel." The older black lady had always been pleasant and helpful during her many visits. "I'd like to see my mother first, though."

With an efficient bob of her head, Mabel called down for an orderly to escort her to her room.

"I'll let Dr. Cavanaugh know that you're here."

Ramona nodded and followed the attendant down the hall to the first-floor room with a view of the grounds. He opened the door for her and she walked in.

Her mother was in a comfortable rocker by the windows facing the gardens, her back to the door. A nurse was at her side, patting her mom on the shoulder as she said, "That's wonderful, Anita. Wonderful."

As the woman saw Ramona, she forced a smile, patted her again and said, "You have a visitor, Anita. Ramona is here."

It was a bad day, Ramona realized immediately.

She walked to her mother's side and pulled up a chair. As she met the nurse's gaze, she noted the kindness and concern there and mouthed a thank-you.

The woman nodded and left her alone with the shell of what had once been her lively and vivacious mother. Ramona slipped her hand over Anita's where it rested on the arm of the rocker. Nothing hinted that she even sensed her touch.

Anita just stared straight ahead at the gardens, a blank, distant look on her face.

Tears threatened and Ramona's throat choked up from the emotion she suppressed. She wouldn't allow sadness to intrude on their time together, so instead, she sat by the rocker and told her mother all about the new paintings she had done and the show Diego had arranged. She skipped possibly being part of an art fraud, and instead focused on her plans for the gallery opening in barely a week.

She even allowed herself to fantasize for a moment, describing what she might wear and how

Diego would notice her, how he'd spend the night at her side and maybe even take her for a celebratory drink after. And then who knew?

Ramona talked until she was almost hoarse, but she doubted her mother even heard a word.

When she looked at her watch, she realized she had been there for nearly two hours, and Dr. Cavanaugh might be waiting for her. Rising, she dropped a kiss on her mother's cheek. The skin was familiar against her lips, and her *mami*'s smell that of her youth. Ramona had made a point of getting her mother's favorite cologne and had requested the nurses use it as a way to try and keep her mind focused on familiar things.

It was the reason that many of the items that had once been in their Spanish Harlem apartment were now in her mother's room. Her parents' wedding pictures. School photos of Ramona at various ages. Some other photos of distant cousins, since both of Ramona's parents had been only children, leaving her without much immediate family.

Near the door, Ramona stopped to call the front desk to find out if Dr. Cavanaugh was still available. Minutes later she entered his office, and the kindly older man smiled and stood. He walked over and hugged her hard, everything about his demeanor calm and soothing.

He guided her to a couch at the side of his office and he sat down beside her, holding her hand as he spoke.

"How are you, Ramona? You're looking well today," he said, his gaze inquisitive as he examined her.

"I'm fine, Dr. Cavanaugh. How's *mami* doing?" she asked, not that she needed to be told her condition was growing worse. Despite that, his report still saddened her.

"Anita's condition is deteriorating rapidly. Her moments of awareness and lucidity are fewer and fewer."

Ramona thought of her mom, vacantly sitting in the chair, her mind gone but her body alive. Quite the opposite of her own state. Ironic.

"How long before…"

Dr. Cavanaugh gently squeezed her hand. "Before she can no longer function at all? Not long, unfortunately."

Ramona sucked in a shaky breath, battling to remain calm. "The trust fund I've set up… It will be enough to take care of her for some time, right?"

"You needn't worry about that. Concentrate on getting better yourself," he said, and Ramona didn't have the heart to tell him that there was nothing she could do to make herself better. All she could do was prolong her life just a little bit more. Just enough to make the money she needed to guarantee her mother would be cared for when she was gone.

"I will, Dr. Cavanaugh. I'll be back soon to see *mami*," she said, but as she left his office she sensed his scrutiny and knew he hadn't been fooled by her words.

They both knew her promise to return might be an empty one.

Chapter 4

Deranged Artist Stalks Rich Millionaire. More on the news at ten. Ramona could not stop the odd thoughts as the two guards at the entrance to the van Winter building watched her closely, their hands crossed before them in that practiced pose law enforcement types must learn in a class called How to Look Menacing 101.

She'd been calling for days, but her many requests to speak to Mr. van Winter all met with the same response: he was in a meeting and couldn't be disturbed.

Quite a difference from his behavior during the six months she had been busy copying the paintings. Then the reclusive millionaire would visit her at least twice a day to check on her progress and comment on her artistic abilities. The time they'd shared had alleviated some of her concerns about his reasons for copying the paintings.

Coming down to the building to try to speak to him hadn't helped at all. She wasn't on any approved-visitors list, and calls to van Winter's assistant revealed that the woman was no longer with the company.

With determination, Ramona swept her gaze up the gleaming metal-and-glass structure of Van Winter Enterprises and thought, *If Mohammed won't come to the mountain, I'll just bring the mountain to Mohammed.*

Julio Vasquez strolled from painting to painting, stroking his goateed chin with long, elegant fingers while Diego stood by patiently, waiting for his old friend's opinion.

"Brilliant!" he said, and whirled to face him, his arms stretched wide. "Absolutely brilliant. I can see why you would toss me aside for these gems, *amigo*."

Theatrical as always, Diego thought. He approached and laid his arm across Julio's shoulders. "You know I would never toss you aside, but—"

"You have feelings for the *señorita*," Julio teased.

Diego tried to defuse any further inquiry. "I believe in her work, Julio. Nothing more."

With a flamboyant swish of his hand, Julio

slipped from beneath his arm and walked to stand before one of the paintings again. After a moment, he called over his shoulder, "She desires, you as well. It's here, *amigo*. In her work. Can you not see it?"

Diego stepped up beside his friend and examined the painting once again, the one he had stood before a few nights ago with Ramona at his side..The one that had led to that rather interesting, but ill-advised, encounter.

Once again he noted the loving sweep of the brush across the woman's hip, the possessive strokes delineating the man's arm as it wrapped around her waist. He tracked the line of that arm up to the indistinct face.

He had thought Ramona had left the man virtually faceless as her way of allowing the observer to complete the canvas in his or her own mind. Now, though, prompted by Julio's words, he noticed the familiar line of the jaw, the way the hair—longish and of a similar color to his—fell forward as his might if he cupped her hips to him and bent his head to taste the flesh of her neck.

"Dios mio, amigo," Julio said with a strangled breath, and Diego suddenly realized that with his friend's vampire abilities, he would pick up on that thrum of power that sexual desire created in their kind.

"I have not felt that from you since Esperanza," his old friend said, for Julio had been with him for so long. Had been instrumental in giving him the eternal life he now had.

Regret filled Diego as he remembered the events that had forever changed his world.

A shadow wavered before him, waking him.

"Esperanza?"

He opened his eyes, but instead encountered an old friend—another nobleman and an aspiring artist with whom he regularly shared a cup or two.

"Don Julio." He lacked the strength to say more or ask how the lordly painter had managed to get past the guards. The torture earlier that day had sapped what little life was left in Diego.

"Amigo, you have managed to create quite a stir with your refusal to confess." Don Julio helped him into a sitting position.

"I am innocent," he said, but found it hard to speak due to the weakness in his body.

"You may be, but that won't save you. Your wife and her lover are dying from a fever. Some say it is the devil's work."

Don Julio knelt beside him, and as the moonlight played across his old friend's face, Diego noted it looked ashen, almost otherworldly in the pale glow.

"Are you well?" Diego asked, concerned for his friend.

"Never better, unlike you. You are to be burned alive in a few days. They prepare for an immense auto de fé in the plaza."

So he was to die a public spectacle in the town square, deprived of dignity up to the very last second of his life? If there was any consolation, it was that his wife and her lapdog of a lover might shortly follow him to hell for what they had done.

"Gracias, amigo, *for the news."*

Don Julio hesitated, and a glimmer of anxiety swept across his features before he said, "I bring more than news. I bring a chance for life."

"Life?"

"Life such as you can't imagine, Diego. Are you brave enough to take the chance?"

Diego thought of the vows he had made to himself in the last month. Of all the dreams he had yet to fulfill. Of Esperanza, with her kind eyes and gentle touch. Of how he had yet to properly thank her for all she'd done for him.

"Sí, *I am brave enough."*

His friend nodded, and Diego watched with fascination and horror as the dark brown of Julio's eyes bled out to an oddly glowing blue-green. He was so fascinated by the change that for a second he failed to notice the long fangs descending from Don Julio's mouth.

"Madre de Dios," *he said, shocked by the transformation. But he didn't flinch as his friend bent toward him.*

If anything, he bared his neck, wanting to make the task easier. The brush of his friend's lips against his skin was a shock, an almost loving gesture before the bite and its pain. But soon after, the distress receded, followed by passion that made him hold Julio's head to him, wanting his embrace never to end.

But it did, as his eyesight dimmed from the loss of blood, and Julio whispered against his ear, "Bite me."

The fever of the vampire transformation had racked his body with alternating chills and fever for over a day before imprisoning him in a world of darkness from which he fought to escape. When he finally woke, he found himself tightly bound in foul-smelling sheets. Struggling against the fabric, he rent it with his hands and emerged, only to find Julio kneeling beside him, knife in hand.

"Always the impatient one," his friend teased, but then his look grew serious. "They discovered Esperenza was helping you. She's to be burned alive tomorrow. We must hurry."

After cutting away the rest of the linens, Julio rose and led Diego along the edges of the building the Inquisitor had turned into his prison. At the back, Julio paused at the entrance to a root cellar, where a large boulder blocked the thick wooden door. Julio lifted the immense stone as if it weighed nothing. At Diego's questioning glance, his friend whispered, "You will soon be able to test your own powers."

They entered the cellar and then the basement storage areas that had been converted into holding cells for the sinners awaiting punishment.

A few doors down, Julio halted and pointed at one cell. Diego peered in through the bars.

Esperanza lay on the ground, sprawled across the dirt and straw. A rat rooted around her skirts, but she seemed either unaware or uncaring. He whispered her name, but she didn't move, creating the fear in him that she had already slipped from life.

"Esperanza," he whispered again, but she didn't stir.

He grabbed the lock with his hands and, remembering Julio's earlier words and action, violently twisted it. It bent as if made of putty, and he quickly removed it and made his way to Esperanza's side.

Her eyes were closed, but as he laid his hand on her cold cheek, they fluttered open. "I heard you call my name. I thought it was a dream."

A wisp of a smile crept across her lips before her eyes fluttered shut again.

He placed his hands on the pulse point of her neck and noted how weak and thready it was. Cursing beneath his breath, he cradled her to his chest, wanting to offer the comfort of his body's warmth, only he had no warmth to give. He had nothing to give her except the love he had come to feel for her and the kiss that Julio had offered him. Diego wanted her to have another chance at life. A life in which they could explore their burgeoning love.

Cradling her cheek, he managed to rouse her

again, her expressive brown eyes sparking with a bit of life. "Diego. You're truly here," she said weakly.

"Amor, *I'm here for you. Will you come with me?" He brushed his hand across the matted strands of her once luxuriant auburn locks.*

"I am yours, Diego. Forever."

He waited no longer.

With the instinct of the demon's blood now flowing through his veins, he called forth the beast. Heat pooled at the center of him and sped outward, charging his body as everything around him came to even sharper focus. Hunger rose, needing appeasement, and in answer, he sensed the fangs slipping downward, heard the erratic beat of her heart, urging him to act before death called.

He bent his head, and shivered at the first brush of his fangs against her pulse point. Dragging in one last breath, he whispered, "Forgive me, mi amor," *and plunged his teeth into her neck.*

Chapter 5

Ramona had already prepared for a few openings in her short career as an artist, and they always filled her with excitement. This visit to the gallery to check things out was no different and possibly even more compelling, since it would likely be her last.

The gallery was closed to the public in anticipation of the showing, which was now only two nights away. She was anxious to see how Diego had placed her paintings and decorated the space, since he always seemed to find just the right way to highlight the chosen works.

She was filled with trepidation at one other thing she planned to do that night—ask Diego for the phone number of one of the buyers from the van Winter auction. She knew he had it because the woman in question was a frequent visitor to his gallery and had, in fact, bought one of Ramona's earlier works.

Although Ramona didn't plan on calling the woman right away, she hoped that letting van Winter know that she was in possession of the number would spur him to see her and answer some of her questions. She didn't want to consider what she would do if he ignored her request.

The buyer might consent to speak with her, but then what? The woman would likely think Ramona crazy if she accused van Winter of putting a forgery up for sale. Worse, the accusations would impact on Diego, and that was the last thing she wanted to happen.

Diego had been too good to her, and she didn't want to hurt him in any way.

Slowly she climbed the three short steps to the exclusive Soho gallery. A rich satin drape with a fanciful crest and Diego's name blocked the main display window. She rapped on the glass door with her knuckle and a light snapped on in one of the back rooms. A second later, Diego strolled out.

He was dressed casually in black jeans and a charcoal-gray sweater that seemed painted to his body. Seeing her at the door, he rushed to open it.

"I hope you haven't been waiting long." He took

her hand and noticed the cold once again, much like a few nights before.

"Not long." She eased her hand from his and rubbed it self-consciously as she stepped into the gallery and looked around, clearly eager to see how he had prepared for the showing.

Diego did not plan on rushing the surprise. "Let's get you comfortable." He slipped his hands to her shoulders and eased off her coat, tossing it on a chair. Then he walked to a long table set in the anteroom, where a lone bottle of wine sat beside two glasses. "At the show we'll have some refreshments here before we direct everyone inside to the main displays," he explained.

Ramona flicked a finger in the direction of the central exhibit area of the gallery. "When can I see?"

Diego chuckled, approached her and cupped her cheek. "Some things shouldn't be rushed, little one," he teased, determined to make everything perfect for her. He ignored the voice in his head that said becoming personally involved with her was a mistake.

For starters, she was human. And beautiful. A definite strike against her. The last beautiful woman he had become involved with had betrayed him and cost him his mortal life. He knew little about Ramona, but he had seen the shadows of secrets in her eyes.

The yearning in the paintings, however, and the

possibility that he had produced such hunger, overrode common sense and caution.

He eased his hand over hers, urging her toward the table. He poured the wine and offered her a glass, which she accepted, then held up his own in a toast. "To our successful partnership."

"To success." She clinked her glass with his, took a sip and smiled. "Very good."

"Just like your paintings," he said, and walked to the entryway leading to the main exhibit area. With the hand holding the glass, he flipped a switch, illuminating the space beyond.

Intrigued, Ramona stepped to the opening and gasped at the sight of her paintings on display.

Diego had hung them simply, without even the benefit of frames, as if to do so would somehow inhibit the motion in the paintings. On the first wall were a trio of her smaller studies. Two mouths barely brushing against each other. A pair of hands, fingers intertwined. The curve of a breast with a hand cupping its weight.

The temperature in the room seemed to rise as she recalled the inspiration for those paintings. Diego. His hands. His lips. His long, elegant fingers, those of an artist and not a businessman. Which made her wonder about the man standing beside her…

"They look wonderful. So tell me, how did you decide that this was your life's calling?"

Diego's mouth thinned into a tight line and he turned away from her. Cradling his glass in his fingers, he pointed to her work. "I dabbled in the art world for a long time until the death of someone I knew convinced me that works like these needed a voice. A champion."

Passionate, but a nonanswer, Ramona thought. She was aware of the various artists he had supported in this gallery, but wondered about the others before his arrival in New York. "You've been here for what? Ten years now?"

"So many questions. Why tonight?" he said and without waiting for her reply, walked to the next viewing room in the gallery.

She followed silently considering how to broach the one question sure to pique his interest. For the moment, however, she allowed herself to be a spectator to her art. As before, the images of the couples in the paintings moved her.

Taking a sip of her wine, she strolled to the last room in the gallery. Her gaze skipped over the two smaller pieces on one wall and focused on the largest of her works, clearly the one Diego intended as the centerpiece of the showing. It was the one she and Diego had examined nearly a week ago. The one that had led to their first kiss.

Her hand shook as she gulped a bracing mouthful of wine.

Diego came to stand beside her, sipping his own wine slowly, gracefully, his movements fluid and sophisticated as always.

"It will fetch a nice sum, but I imagine you will

be sad to see it go," he said, apparently misinterpreting the reason for her yearning.

She half turned and gave in to the need that had been building since the other night. She cradled his jaw, slipped her thumb over his lips wet with wine. "Sometimes there are things more important than money."

More than most, Diego knew the truth of that statement. Honor. Duty. Love. All things more important than the lucre most humans were so greedy to hoard. That she understood that brought hope that she wasn't like his wife. That she was the kind of woman who could be trusted.

He somehow divested them of the wineglasses, laid his hand over hers and stroked the soft skin there. He took a step closer to her and bent his head, whispering as he did so, "I hope this is one of them."

He kissed her as he had been longing to since a few days ago, exploring the edges of her lips, slipping his tongue past the seam of her mouth to taste her.

It wasn't enough, he thought, dropping his hand to her shoulder and tracing the fine lines of her collarbone. From there he followed the gap at the collar of her shirt, brushing his fingers against the soft skin there before cupping her breast.

Beneath his palm her nipple crested into a hard peak, and he couldn't resist. He took the tip between his thumb and forefinger and gently rotated it, dragging a ragged gasp from her.

It urged him onward, and he dipped his head to the crook of her neck, where her pulse beat erratically. Inhaling, he brought her scent into his memory and dropped a kiss at the juncture, resisting the demon's urge to bite and feed.

The human wanted to bite something else much, much more.

Ramona should have protested as he quickly undid the front of her blouse, parting the fabric to reveal the lace bra beneath. With a deft flick of his wrist, he undid the front clasp and her full breasts spilled free, allowing him access. For a fleeting moment, she considered withdrawing, until he closed his mouth over her nipple, sucking it into his mouth. She moaned and cupped his head to her urgently. The reality of Diego as a lover was more than she had dreamed, and she set aside all reservations to allow herself this special moment.

When she moaned, the sound vibrated deep within Diego, stirring his soul. He forced away all doubts about the wisdom of this. About how little he knew of Ramona and how little she knew of him.

Such as the fact that he was a vampire.

The thought sobered him, quenching the sharp desire that had risen so swiftly between them.

Slowly, regretfully, he tempered his caresses, rearranged her bra and shirt and eased away. But he kept his connection with her by grasping her hand. "I'm sorry. I didn't mean for this to happen again."

"Me, neither," she replied, and gently eased her hand from his. "Maybe we need to think about whether we should keep it just business between us."

What Ramona said made sense, but something inside of him wanted to challenge her too-logical suggestion. "Business?" He motioned to the canvas on the wall, pressing his point. "Is that what you imagined between us when you created that painting?"

A wide range of emotions roiled through her, chief among them embarrassment that he had seen through the images on the canvas to the passion that had driven her to paint it. That discovery had exposed her soul.

The need to flee overwhelmed her. Ramona raced from the room, pausing only to grab her coat and slip it on. Somehow, Diego beat her to the door in a blur of speed and blocked her way.

"I didn't mean to embarrass you."

"But you did." She placed a hand on his chest to urge him aside, but he remained firmly in position, preventing her from leaving.

"I'm sorry," he stressed again, and laid his hand on her shoulder in a gesture meant to comfort. "What can I do to make it up to you?" he added, almost as an afterthought.

It wasn't how she had imagined raising the issue. In fact, as the night had progressed, she had almost forgotten what she would ask of him. But now that the moment had presented itself, she couldn't ignore the opportunity.

"I need a favor."

Diego scrolled through the contacts on his PDA, prolonging the moment with the hope of discovering just what Ramona wanted. The request for Alicia Tipton's phone number had caught him off guard, and Ramona's failure to provide any reason for the request troubled him greatly.

It wasn't just that Alicia was a valued client and had helped put his gallery on the map by referring her rich and famous friends to him. He sensed Ramona's worry, but her lack of trust in him created worry of his own.

The promise he had made himself so long ago reared up—to never place his faith in another beautiful woman. He had trusted his wife and she had betrayed him.

Would Ramona do the same? Was she asking for the phone number for something less than trustworthy?

He paused, the stylus poised over the PDA screen and the entry for Alicia's number as he stared across his desk to where Ramona sat, waiting. She fidgeted with one sleeve of her coat, clearly nervous.

He pressed for an answer once again. "Why do you need Alicia's number?"

"I would understand if you don't want to give it

to me. I know she's an important patron of this gallery."

"She'll be here on Friday night. I could introduce you to her then."

Ramona flinched under his intense gaze. "It's okay. Don't worry," she said, but everything about her seemed to deflate, as if his refusal had sucked all the life out of her.

He couldn't stand to see her spirit falter like that, and even though common sense and his long-ago vow warned him not to do it, he opened the contact entry for Alicia and copied the number down on a slip of paper.

Holding it out, he said, "Here it is. Don't make me regret that I gave it to you."

"I won't, Diego. I promise you that I would never do anything to hurt you." Ramona took the small piece of paper, folded it and slipped it into her coat pocket as she rose from the chair.

He examined her carefully, knowing her well enough to see that she was greatly troubled. No doubt it was about the reason she needed Alicia's number.

Protectiveness welled up in him, which should have set off warning bells about the idiocy of having any feelings for her other than distrust. But he couldn't forget how she stirred him. How her passion called to him after he'd felt alone for so long.

He didn't want to admit it, but the last few centuries with Esperanza, while entertaining, had at times been trying and difficult as he strove to fulfill her needs.

He suspected Ramona was quite a different creature that way—able to take care of herself and independent enough to constantly challenge any man lucky to be in her life. She was passionate and caring, judging both from her paintings and his voyeuristic visit as she'd satisfied her needs. Diego was certain that any life with Ramona would be intensely rewarding.

And because of that, he ignored all the sensible warnings coming from his inner voice and asked, "Would you like to have dinner with me?"

Chapter 6

Ramona didn't want to think about dying. She had woken this morning feeling more alive than she had in weeks. Last night with Diego, as frustrating as it had been on some levels, had sparked a fire within her, creatively and emotionally.

Dinner had been pleasant, both the food and the company. They had kept it to business at first, but as they walked out of the restaurant, Diego had reached for her hand, the action cautious but promising.

At the door to her apartment she had been tempted to invite him in and continue what they had started in the gallery. Common sense had reared its head, however. They had shared some kisses, which began chastely but ended with them straining against each other, wanting more.

That want now manifested itself on the paper in her hands. With fast, efficient strokes, she began the charcoal sketch. She might not have time to complete it in oils, she realized, but soon forced such negative thoughts from her mind.

The general outline of the drawing took shape as she sketched quickly. She was intent on drawing when her cell phone rang. She didn't recognize the number, but answered. "Ramona Escobar."

"We seem to have a problem, Ms. Escobar," Frederick van Winter stated. "I'll drop by your loft at twelve today." And with that, he ended the call.

Ramona smiled. Her ploy of faxing him Alicia Tipton's number had worked. Van Winter was coming to her just as she had wanted.

Now she had to think about what she would do with him once he got there.

The familiar clunk and clang of the refurbished warehouse elevator provided an early warning system for arriving guests. Ramona pulled open the large rolling door precisely at twelve, as the elevator deposited Frederick van Winter at her doorstep.

"Ms. Escobar," he said with a polite nod of his silvery head.

"Mr. van Winter. So good of you to come," she said, and gestured to the entry to her loft.

With another nod, he strolled in, the aroma of an

expensive cologne wafting past her. From the soft leather soles of his handmade Italian shoes to the Savile Row suit and stylishly trimmed hair, van Winter was the picture of understated sophistication and old money.

Possibly other people's money, Ramona reminded herself as she pulled the door closed and stepped forward to guide him toward her kitchen table. She had laid out coffee and tea in the hopes they could discuss the apparent misunderstanding civilly, but van Winter stalked past the table into the center of the loft.

Glancing around the large space, with its industrial-style lighting and rough brick walls, he seemed displeased, until he turned and noted the charcoal sketch on her easel. The morning light streamed in from the skylights above, casting a natural glow on the half-finished portrait of Diego. She had wanted to immortalize the look on his face after he had kissed her last night.

Van Winter brushed his hand across the edge of the paper, murmuring, "Is this someone I know? He looks familiar."

"I don't believe you do," she said, and motioned to the rough-hewn oak kitchen table with its place settings. "Would you care for some coffee?"

"I'm trying to understand why you faxed me Alicia Tipton's phone number. As a threat, maybe?"

Van Winter didn't budge from his spot before her easel, making it clear he would be in control. But she wasn't about to be cowed by him. Her honor was all she had left, and nothing would stop her from clearing her name. She took a seat at the table and poured herself some coffee as she explained her concerns.

"I saw the paintings that you put up for auction. *My* copies. Not the originals."

Van Winter didn't look her way as he said, "We used your copies for security reasons. We felt it best to keep the masters in one place until it was time for them to go to the buyers."

She had thought of that as a possible excuse herself, but nothing about van Winter's actions since the auction had allayed her fears. If anything, his avoidance of her during the last few days spoke volumes to the contrary.

"I'm glad to hear that. It will be nice to see the original when I personally deliver my painting to Ms. Tipton. She's apparently quite interested in one of my new works," Ramona bluffed. Satisfaction filled her when tension stiffened van Winter's body.

He turned and approached the table, then tightly gripped the top rung of one of the chairs. "Don't play with me, Ramona."

Barely suppressed rage laced his words, and above his pristine white collar, a telltale flush crept up his neck.

"Why did you do it?" she challenged, her hands wrapped around her coffee cup to keep her own anger at bay. In her youth, she might have resorted to violence, but she had learned that calm was sometimes a more effective weapon in a fight.

"I had no choice but to sell the paintings. I had borrowed from the foundation and needed to make things right before the auditors discovered what I like to call a 'personal loan.'

"I knew I was going to miss them, and needed something to hang in their place, so I thought, why not have copies made?"

"Why me?" she asked, and took a sip of her coffee.

"An associate visited some local art schools and noticed your name on a project."

A smile came to his face, and its malevolence leached up to his cold, silver-gray eyes. "You're a dead woman walking. Even the copies will be valuable one day."

He moved away then, his stride brisk and almost joyful. "How important is it to you that your mother stays well? What will it take to make the last months of your own life more comfortable?"

Her coffee cup rattled against the saucer as she battled her rage. She released the cup, laid her hands on the table and slowly rose, counting to ten before she walked to the door and pulled it open.

"I believe we're done here, Mr. van Winter."

He chuckled and shook his head. "You're not understanding me, Ms. Escobar."

Walking toward her, he paused at the door and looked down at her from his slightly greater height.

"Say a word to anyone...*anyone* about your mistaken impressions, and you and your mother might find the rest of your lives quite difficult."

As she met his gaze, Ramona realized that all of his wealth and trappings couldn't hide the evil in his heart. She knew then that he wouldn't hesitate to make good on his threat. The realization created a chill deep within her. But she knew she couldn't back down from bullies like van Winter.

"Touch my mother and you will regret the day you were born, Frederick. I'm a dead woman walking, remember, and I've got nothing to lose by taking you down."

He lost all his bluster and bravado then, and stormed to the elevator. But she didn't wait to see him leave before yanking the door shut.

She leaned against it and took in a deep breath, her body shaking from the delayed reaction of the confrontation. A cold knot of fear tightened in her gut as she considered his parting words.

He was a rich and powerful man with all kinds of connections. Could he really harm her mother?

Ramona wasn't about to take the risk, but didn't know whom she could trust. Diego? Would he believe her? Could he help her?

Walking to the easel, she glanced at the portrait she had begun. She imagined that the passion she already saw in it was real. That he would actually care what became of her. Only she didn't dare hope.

* * *

Diego hated the nervous butterflies that danced in his stomach as he double-checked every single inch of the gallery space. He wanted it to be perfect for Ramona.

He stalked to the anteroom, where the guests would mingle for refreshments and his staff would process inquiries or sales of Ramona's paintings. Diego suspected there would be quite a few of the latter.

Nervously rubbing his hands together, he took a last look at the paintings in each room, making sure they were hanging just so and that the lighting created the proper effect. Satisfied with the displays in the first two rooms, he moved to the last, and to his favorite painting. The one he regretfully knew would fetch the highest price. The one he should have kept for himself, only doing so would have been like an act of self-flagellation, reminding him of all that he desired but couldn't have.

He was standing there, admiring the painting one last time, when someone slapped a hand on his back.

"It's not good to pine, Diego," Julio quipped. "Why not just end your misery and put the bite on her?"

Diego glanced around and saw they were alone in the room. "Who let you in?"

With a theatrical wave of his wrist, Julio said, "You know I'm irresistible when I want to be."

Unlike Diego, Julio was not above using his vamp powers for his own benefit or amusement. A subtle suggestion coupled with a blast of undead energy could accomplish quite a lot. Together with a shot of vamp speed, it would explain how Julio had crashed the opening. Which prompted Diego to remind his friend, "No more antics tonight."

"What? No biting?" he questioned with an exaggerated pout, although both of them knew Julio would not risk exposure by fully morphing before a crowd.

Diego was about to answer when his vamp senses picked up on a familiar scent. "I've got to go. Behave yourself."

Despite his warning to Julio, Diego put on a burst of vampire acceleration and arrived at the anteroom just as one of his staff was about to help Ramona with her jacket. Diego stepped in, slipping his hands to her shoulders to remove the serviceable peacoat, which he passed to a clerk.

What she wore was anything but serviceable, Diego thought as his eyes took in the deep wine-colored velvet gown that artfully draped the slender lines of her body and the generous curves of her breasts. Silver combs pulled her thick chestnut hair back from her face, highlighting the fine bones there.

"*Felicidades,*" he whispered against her ear, wishing her well.

Ramona faced him and smiled, but she seemed tired and even more pale than she had the other day. "*Gracias,* Diego. I didn't realize it was you."

"Where else should I be but at your side?" He slipped his arm through hers and urged her to the bar, where he snared two glasses of red wine. He handed her one and raised his in a toast. "To a fine showing. I know it will be a success."

"Again, *gracias*. It wouldn't have been possible without you."

Diego nodded, sipped his wine and then shot a quick look at his watch. "We're going to open the doors soon. Are you ready?"

Was she? Ramona wondered, risking a look at Diego, who was peering at her a little too intently. She recalled their kisses after dinner and how they'd both moved away from their just-business vow. What would tonight bring? she wondered, and guilt rose sharply again.

She was lying to him with each kiss, promising more than she could ever give.

"Ramona?" he murmured, as if sensing something was amiss.

"Diego, I—"

She didn't get to finish, for the doors to the gallery opened and the first few guests had entered.

"Excuse me," Diego said and with a brush of his hand against hers, headed to the door to greet his customers and assorted guests.

She needed a moment to collect herself before she met any prospective buyers. Normally she was undaunted by such meet and greets, but the importance of tonight, on so many levels, had her nerves shot. Not to mention that yesterday's emotional turmoil at van Winter's visit had robbed her of most of a night's sleep.

Rushing to the back room, she found Julio Vazquez there, intently studying her large painting. As she entered, he turned and shot her a knowing smile.

"It's a masterpiece. How can you part with it?" he asked with a flourish of his hand. He approached her and floated air kisses above each of her cheeks.

"*Gracias,* Julio. I didn't know you'd be coming tonight." Diego was generally good about advising when another of his artists would be dropping by; it helped keep some of the egos at bay, not that she was bothered by Julio's presence, although there was something particularly catty about his attitude at the moment.

"*Amiga,* how could I miss the showing that bumped mine?"

She peered at him, eyes narrowed to slits. "What do you mean, 'bumped mine'?"

"Come now, *niña.* Isn't it obvious that he's, well…flattered by your attentions?"

Ramona bade Julio a frosty goodbye. Then she went in search of Diego, who had lied about the sudden opening in his schedule. She hadn't wanted the money he'd offered, and she certainly hadn't wanted him to pull anyone else's show on her behalf.

She didn't need anyone thinking that he was playing favorites, she thought as she entered the second display room and noticed Diego standing beside Alicia Tipton. The older woman's head was bent toward him as he gestured to the trio of pictures, her interest half on the paintings and half on Diego.

Clearly Ramona would have to wait until later to discuss Julio's comments. Much later, she realized as she scanned the gallery and noticed the crowd that had gathered.

Diego must have spotted her, for he held up his hand and gestured for her to come over. When she'd made her way through the throng, he introduced her to Mrs. Tipton. Diego was about to make a more public introduction when a low buzz of excitement crept through the room, drawing everyone's attention to the door of the gallery.

Frederick van Winter stood there, regally debonair. On either side of him stood beefy bodyguards, making it obvious to anyone who didn't recognize the reclusive millionaire that this was someone to be noticed. As he stepped forward, the crowd parted like the Red Sea before Moses.

Crossing the room, he stretched out his arm to Mrs. Tipton, "Alicia, it's been way too long," he said, bending over her hand and kissing it.

"It's a shame you've been hiding yourself lately," she responded with a titter before introducing Diego.

"Mr. Rivera. I've heard quite a bit about your gallery. This creature beside you is the artist, I assume," he said, so smoothly that for a moment Ramona almost believed his charade.

"Mr. van Winter." Her tone came across a bit curt, earning a puzzled look from Diego, who quickly tried to smooth things over.

"I'd be delighted to show you some of Ms. Escobar's works," he said obsequiously, bowing slightly and holding his hand out in invitation.

Van Winter ignored the gesture and instead offered his arm to Ramona. "Ms. Escobar, I'd prefer if you gave me a private tour. That is, if you don't mind my spiriting her away, Rivera."

An angry look crossed Diego's face for a moment before he schooled his emotions. With a solicitous nod, he said, "Of course not. *Mi casa es su casa.*"

She wasn't a house, Ramona wanted to shout. She was a woman. A woman with a mind of her own who didn't want to have to pretend to enjoy Frederick van Winter's company. But of course, she couldn't make a scene in front of all these people.

Van Winter walked her to the farthest room in the gallery, where he paused and nodded to his two goons. With quiet and menacing efficiency they emptied the room, until only she and van Winter remained. Then they blocked the entryway with their bodies.

She yanked her hand from his arm and rubbed at it, as if trying to wipe away something dirty.

Van Winter seemed amused by her actions, but then focused on the large painting, moving forward and backward, then to one side as he studied it.

"Quite magnificent," he began. "I may have to acquire it for my collection, especially since it will soon be worth so much more."

Dead artists' works always fetched higher prices, Ramona knew, but she didn't allow his comment to faze her. Instead she said, "What are you doing here?"

"Enjoying a rare night out. That's not a crime, as far as I know, but maybe you would know better about crime."

Slimy bastard, she thought, but forced a smile to her lips. "I don't know why you came—"

"To see if you are truly an artist or just a master at copying." He once again scrutinized the painting, and was about to place a finger on the canvas when she snagged his hand.

"Don't." She couldn't bear to have him soil the work with his touch.

Van Winter switched his attention to her, with a cold, almost snakelike smile. "I didn't realize just how much it meant to you. How much *he* means to you."

From behind them came the sounds of a struggle, and as she released van Winter's hand, she noticed Diego breaking past the two guards. He rushed to her side. "Is everything all right?"

Van Winter looked from her to Diego to the painting, and his smile grew broader. "Just fine. I'm going to look at the other paintings before I make up my mind which one to buy."

"Of course, but please remember there are other guests here, as well. I can't have your bodyguards intimidating my patrons," Diego said.

With a nod of acquiescence, van Winter waved for his goons to depart, and then followed them out.

Diego turned to her, his expression grim. "Mind telling me what's going on?"

Chapter 7

Ramona wrapped her arms around herself and stalked to the far side of the room, her back to him. When she whirled around, her anger was palpable in the taut set of her body and the tight slash of her lips.

"I might ask the same thing. What's going on? You lied to me."

Tonight was not going the way he'd imagined, Diego decided, from the hermit millionaire's surprise visit to Ramona's accusations. "What are you talking about?"

She walked back to him and jabbed a finger in his chest. "Julio told me that you bumped his show for mine. Is that true?"

Damn him, Diego thought. In the nearly five

hundred years they had known each another, it had never really sunk in with Julio that all Diego wanted to be was a friend and nothing more. He had no doubt that Julio had spilled the beans to cause problems.

"I did ask Julio for a favor, but if he had said no—"

"We both know Julio would never say no to you, Diego. I don't need you saving me. I can take care of myself," she said, emphasizing the point with one last sharp jab of her finger against his chest.

He snagged her hand, and because some of the patrons had started to filter back into the room, he led her to a far corner. Leaning close, he whispered, "Did van Winter upset you?"

"What if he did?" she replied with a tired sigh.

It had been so much easier in the old days, he thought as he cupped her jaw and raised her face to his. "I could call him out for you. Pistols at dawn. Or would you prefer swords?" he teased, almost half wishing he could uphold her honor in such a fashion.

But then, of course, he could just go suck the old bastard dry, if he had done anything truly serious.

"This isn't something to kid about, Diego. The guy's a creep and you're not much better," she said. Then she pushed past him and stormed off.

But as he followed her to the next room, he noted van Winter watching them. Noticed the tightness that entered Ramona's posture whenever the wealthy old man caught her eye. Something was up between the two of them. Something big, Diego realized, and he was quite relieved when van Winter finally left for the night after plunking down a large sum for one of the smaller paintings. The tension his two muscle-bound cretins had created evaporated upon their departure, brightening the night.

Diego mingled with his guests, talking up the paintings and smiling as he noted that his assistant was writing up sales receipts on several occasions. He wandered to the back room once again, drawn by what he had come to consider "his" painting. Diego hoped it wouldn't sell, so that he could buy it himself.

And what will you do with it? the demon's voice in his head chastised. Sit in front of it and reminisce about the human you once knew? Another one you watched shrivel up and die?

Human fate was no match for a vampire's, Diego admitted to himself. Whether willing or not, he could make Ramona his. But because of the humanity he clung to in his heart, and the vow he had made to be a better man, he refused to heed the demon's call.

Ripping himself away from the painting, he returned to working the crowd.

A couple of hours passed and people slowly filtered out, until finally just his staff and the caterer's remained, and Ramona. She had plopped into one of the few available chairs and seemed totally exhausted.

Grabbing two of the last glasses of champagne,

Diego walked over and held one out to her, but she waved him off. "I've had enough, thanks."

She rose, but wobbled a bit, and he immediately swept his arm around her waist to steady her. "I guess you *have* had enough, little one. Let me walk you out."

With a tired nod, she shot him a grateful smile, their earlier upset of the night seemingly forgotten. At the door of the gallery, he helped her down the three small steps to the cobblestoned street. There was no traffic and only a few parked cars remained on the block.

"I'll call a cab for you," he said, and stepped away from her to head back inside.

He had reached the door of the gallery when one of the parked cars suddenly started to move, accelerating swiftly. Tires squealing and lights off, it headed directly for Ramona, who stood frozen in place.

The car—an unassuming, late-model black sedan—jumped the curb, sending sparks flying as the hubcaps grated against the stone. With a blast of inhuman acceleration, Diego flew off the stoop, wrapped her in his embrace and lifted her out of harm's way. A loud thump followed as the car careened back onto the street and raced away.

He glanced at Ramona as he held her in his arms. She was even more pale than before, with a greenish cast to her face that he recognized well. He had but a moment to help her to the curb, where she lost the contents of her stomach. When she was done, he scooped her up and took her back into the gallery. Her body trembled in his arms and he asked, "Are you okay?"

She nodded, but seemed ready to vomit again. "Just the shock of it, I guess."

Ignoring the puzzled looks of his staff, Diego took Ramona to his office bathroom, where he helped her clean up and splash some cold water on her face. Semirestored, she murmured, "Can you give me a minute?"

He hesitated, not sure she was strong enough to be left alone, but then acquiesced and sat down on the sofa in his office to wait for her. When she joined him, he said, "I'm going to call the police. We should file a report."

"You can't." When her gaze met his, he noticed the fear there, but also determination.

"Mind telling me why not?"

Ramona looked down at her hands and wrung them together nervously. He covered them with one of his, stilling the anxious motion. Without looking at him, she softly said, "Because if you do, bad things may happen to people I care about."

At first Diego wasn't sure whether to believe her, but as she lifted her face and he examined her features, he realized she was deadly serious.

As deadly serious as whomever had been behind the wheel of the car that had nearly run her over earlier.

As he recalled the rather unusual encounter with van Winter, he had no doubt the millionaire was somehow involved in whatever was going on.

"Tell me what's wrong," Diego said. But he was unprepared for the story that spilled from her. A story that was not only difficult to believe, but incomplete. As Ramona relayed the details of all that had happened in the last several months, he got the sense that she was being less than honest.

He had already been betrayed once before and didn't want to believe that Ramona was capable of a similar deceit. The only way to know for sure, however, was to consider that her crazy tale might actually be true, and prove that van Winter had committed fraud.

The plan's only problem was that it also meant accepting that Ramona had committed forgery, albeit unknowingly.

"Why didn't you ask me? If it was only the money—"

"It wasn't just about the money and…I couldn't ask you. I didn't want your pity. I don't want it now." She cocked her head at a challenging angle.

Cradling her jaw, he laid his forehead against hers and said, "What I feel for you is anything but pity, *querida*. Can't you tell?"

Ramona reached up and tangled her hands in his hair, stroking the longish strands as she said, "What you're feeling is lust, because you don't know me well enough to feel anything else."

He lowered his hand to her shoulder, idly traced a pattern on her neck with his thumb. "Then let me get to know you better."

She sighed harshly. "I've just told you that I copied three masterpieces and am possibly on someone's hit list, and you want to get to know me better?"

She bit back the part about being a dead woman walking, which would be sure to cinch the deal and have him running away as fast as he could, as most men would. There were few heroes left in this world.

But Diego was apparently harder to scare away than most. "Together we will figure out what to do about van Winter. Trust me."

Trust him? she thought, finding his request almost impossible to fathom. She examined his features, and saw commitment and caring there. Hope rose in her that maybe she had found one of those few remaining heroes. That maybe he could not only help her prove her innocence, but wouldn't run when he discovered the truth about her life. Her expected-to-be-short life.

Buoyed by his reaction, she decided maybe it was time to let Diego learn a little more about her. She slipped her hand into his and said, "Would you take me home? Come in and have some coffee?"

His broad smile was the only answer she needed.

Diego watched as she puttered around her kitchen, making a pot of coffee. The action seemed so normal and yet tonight was anything but normal.

She had just confessed a great deal to him, but he sensed that she had still held back a part of herself. He hoped that this visit to her home, not as a business partner but as a man, would reveal the part of her that she kept hidden.

Like you'll reveal your own secrets?

He ignored his conscience's warning and trained his attention on Ramona, intrigued despite himself.

She was still dressed in the wine-colored velvet gown, and while she looked gorgeous, it seemed out of place here in her home, where he was used to seeing her in the jeans and T-shirts she usually wore to paint. Rising from his chair, he stood behind her and laid his hands on her shoulders.

The velvet was soft beneath his fingers, but not as soft as her skin might feel.

"Why don't you take this off and get comfortable." Easing his fingers beneath the edge of the velvet jacket, he slipped it off to reveal the creamy expanse of her skin.

On her right shoulder was a tattoo, a rose. His fingertip traced the unpracticed lines of the drawing.

"This is—" But he was cut off.

"Not the best artwork. I…"

Beneath his finger he sensed the slight tension in her body before she continued.

"I was a member of a gang in Spanish Harlem. I had to spend some time in juvie, and the leader decided we needed something to identify us. Since we couldn't wear our colors in the detention hall, she came up with this idea."

"A rose in Spanish Harlem," he said, recalling the line from the once popular song. When he bent and dropped a kiss over the tattoo, her body trembled and she pulled away from him.

"It's not romantic, Diego. I spent months in detention because I was too stupid to get out of the gang before it was too late."

He crossed his arms and watched as she grabbed some spoons and napkins and set them on the table in an effort to avoid him. But he wasn't about to let her. "It's part of what made you what you are, *querida*."

She paused, gripping one of the spoons tightly. "I'm an ex-gang member. No one would believe my word against van Winter's. *No one*."

"I do," he said, although he had his reservations. He believed she had not known about van Winter's planned deception, but he had doubts about why she had made the copies. He sensed there was more to that part than she was letting on.

"You said you had concerns about his request, so why did you do it?" He cupped her shoulders, so small and delicate under his large hands.

"My mom. I needed to make sure I could take care of her," Ramona admitted. But even that confession seemed only partial. There was more she wasn't saying, but he sensed she wouldn't reveal it. At least, not just yet.

He slipped his palms to her back and pulled her close, wrapping his arms around her in a tight hug. She responded, burying her head against his chest. They lingered in the embrace until the sputtering of the coffeemaker reminded them why they were supposedly there together.

As the beep signaled that the brewing was done, she eased away from him, but seemed flustered. "It's kind of late. Coffee's probably not a good idea at this hour."

With his vamp metabolism he would be awake all night, anyway, but the dark circles beneath Ramona's eyes hinted she needed some rest.

"Why don't you get ready for bed," he said, inclining his head in the direction of the large four-poster at the far side of the loft.

"I'll let you out." She was headed to the door when he grabbed her arm to stop her.

She faced him with a confused look and he said, "I'm not going anywhere until I know you're safe."

Chapter 8

"You can't be serious." She tried to pull away, but he held fast, his grip strong, but gentle.

"I am, *querida*. Someone tried to run you over tonight and a psycho millionaire threatened you. Until I know you're safe…"

"You cannot stay the night." With slightly more force, she yanked free of his grasp and stormed into the living room area of the loft, where she plopped down onto the couch.

He followed her and took a spot beside her. After bouncing on the cushions a few times, he said, "This should be comfortable enough."

"Diego, be reasonable. You can't expect me to get any rest while you're—"

"Lying here on your couch? So it is true that you find me irresistible," he teased. Reaching up, he plucked one of the silver combs from her hair, which tumbled down onto her shoulder.

He fingered the loose strands and said, "Go to bed. In the morning we will make some calls and try to find out if van Winter made a switch without anyone noticing."

Ramona wanted to protest, but she knew Diego was intractable once he'd made up his mind about something—in this case, staying the night. The truth was she would feel more secure with him around, given what had happened earlier. Still, she had to salvage a bit of pride.

Removing the other comb, she ran her fingers through her hair and noticed how Diego followed the movement of the waves as they fell to her breasts. Placing her index finger on his chin, she applied subtle pressure to raise his gaze to hers. "Seems to me I'm not the only one with *ganas*."

He laid a finger along the swell of her breast, rubbing it just above the edge of the fabric. "I won't deny *mis ganas*. The wanting is very real, Ramona. But let's see who has the strength to resist whom," he challenged.

Her nipples had tightened with his simple touch, but luckily, the velvet was thick enough to hide her reaction. Knowing retreat was the only way to avoid surrender, she rose and whispered good-night before fleeing to her bed on the far side of the loft.

Diego had heard the stutter of her heart and felt the slight rise in her body temperature before she fled. She had been affected by that one modest caress. He didn't need to imagine how she might respond to more. He had watched her nights ago and experienced her passion from afar, as well as up close and personal. Even now he could recall her soft moans and the sharp little gasp as fulfillment had washed over her.

He wondered whether he could survive the night without touching her. Whether he could resist her, or if he'd find himself in her bed, making a fool of himself with the mistaken belief that he could be a part of her life. Her mortal life, he reminded himself, and tamped down the desire awakening in his loins. A complicated life filled with secrets that should have been ringing warning bells.

His suit jacket suddenly felt constricting, and he rose, yanking it off. A moment later he noticed Ramona slipping into bed, wearing a long nightshirt, probably in deference to his presence. But as he sank back onto the couch and stretched along its length, he recalled the image of her naked. The rosy tips of her breasts tight with desire. Her head thrown back as her release claimed her.

He bit back a groan and did the unthinkable: he called forth the demon to chase away his human desire. To drive away the emotion urging him to rise and go to her bed, make love to her until his name exploded from her lips.

The demon would only want one kind of release—that of her sweet blood against its fangs.

The trace of humanity in Diego's heart was strong enough to resist the demon's desire to take the woman, but possibly not strong enough to resist the human's desire to make love to her. As long as he kept the demon with him, he could resist.

He lay there in vamp mode, his senses energized by his vampire power, aware of every sight, sound and smell of the night. The earthy aroma of the coffee they hadn't drunk, cooling on the counter. The shadows in the kitchen giving way to the moonlight spilling onto Ramona's work area. He fought back images of how that same moonlight would caress her curves and valleys as she slept, but failed to erase them.

His fangs elongated in anticipation, and saliva pooled in his mouth at the call of her blood, pulsing through her body. The demon envisioned her pale skin, inhaled the smell of her, so that he would find her no matter where she might try to hide. Sucking in a deep breath to quell the vampire desires that were growing stronger than he had expected, Diego focused on the beat of her heart, steady and with no sign of slowing.

She was still awake.

Was it because of him? he wondered for only a second, because he didn't dare follow those thoughts further.

Instead, he concentrated on the metallic beams

and braces above him, tracing their shadows and lines in the night until slowly his eyes drifted closed, and sleep claimed him.

The sofa creaked with each subtle movement of his body.

He hadn't been resting well until about an hour ago, when it seemed as if he had finally fallen asleep.

Ramona wished she could do the same, but she was unable to forget that the object of her erotic dreams lay barely thirty feet away on her sofa. Between her legs, damp need throbbed, demanding fulfillment.

To channel that need into something more worthwhile, she escaped the tangled sheets and tiptoed to her work space. After grabbing her sketch pad and pencils, she made her way to the love seat across from where Diego slept.

He sprawled across the cushions, magnificently graceful even in sleep. It was a shame that he had too many clothes on, she thought as she began sketching his pose. One long leg outstretched. The other to the side, creating a vee between his legs.

She dragged her eyes from that spot and upward, along the flat planes of his stomach to where the shirt gaped open to midchest, exposing an enticing amount of flesh and hair that she craved to touch.

She satisfied that yearning by creating the enticing whorls with her pencil on the paper beneath her hand. As they took shape, she paused to smudge the lines with her finger to delineate the hollow between the well-defined muscles of his chest. A chest that still rose smoothly and peacefully in sleep.

Pleased with how the drawing was taking shape, she continued capturing the lines of his body. The broad shoulders straining the fine cotton of his shirt. His arms, one pillowed behind his head and the other resting loosely along his side, palm upward, with his exquisitely long, masculine fingers relaxed in slumber.

She moved upward to his face and stroked the sharp lines of his jaw and cheekbones onto the paper, then sketched in the lock of hair spilling downward.

Glancing at her model once more, she nearly jumped out of her seat as a startling blue-green gleam appeared, before his eyelids fluttered open to reveal the coolness of his ice-blue eyes.

"You're awake," she said with a soft exhalation, afraid to disturb the moment. Afraid to move.

"Make believe I'm not." He closed his eyes once again and maintained his position, but she couldn't fail to miss how strain crept into his muscles.

"Relax," she urged, but he chuckled and peeked at her from beneath his lowered lids.

"Should I be as relaxed as you?" His tones were soft, like a lover's in the night, but tinged with his biting humor.

With the moment fleeing, she dropped her hand into her lap, frustrated at capturing only a part of his grace on the paper. Determined not to lose the inspiration, she said, "Close your eyes and take a breath. Do something to get comfortable again."

Diego wanted to laugh out loud at the thought that he could somehow be at rest with her sitting across from him, naked beneath the nightshirt. In the brief moment before he'd reined in the demon, his vamp eyesight had picked up on the dusky shadows of her nipples beneath the fabric, had smelled the musky dampness of her arousal, begging for him to taste.

Comfortable? he thought, as, between his own legs, human passion awakened once again. He knew there was only one way he could remotely get comfortable.

One hand was pillowed behind his head, but with the other he undid the buttons on his shirt, parting the fabric to let the cool night air wash away the lingering heat. His nipples tightened with the chill and he forced himself not to imagine how it might feel if her warm mouth replaced the nip of the evening.

The scratching of Ramona's pencil against the paper stopped, and he opened his eyes to stare at her.

"You can…take it off if you'd like," she said, gesturing to his shirt.

Even as he slipped off the garment and tossed it aside, he called himself a fool. His passions had gotten him into trouble once before, and tonight was no different, he told himself. But the warning wasn't enough to quench the fire building in his loins. Especially not when Ramona's hungry gaze traced the lines of his muscles, and her hand moved quickly across the paper, rendering those lines in her drawing.

She paused for a moment as her gaze drifted downward, and even in the dark, he detected the becoming flush spreading across her cheeks when she settled her attention on his erection.

He decided to continue with her earlier request. He undid his pants, dragged them and his briefs away, before reclining again on the couch, attempting to resume his original position.

Dios mio, Ramona thought, her hand faltering against the paper, dragging an errant line as he finally revealed himself. She had sketched many a nude model before, but none had been quite as magnificent. She snared the gum eraser from her lap and carefully removed the offensive line, replacing it with the strong sweep of his hip. She darkened one edge to create the shadow at the juncture of his thighs and the tight curls from which his erection jutted.

As before, she traced and blurred the edges with the tip of her finger, her movements more sure against the paper than they could be if it were his flesh beneath her hands.

At that thought she worked quickly, aware of his discomfort as he lay there, aroused. Aware of her own desire to replace the rough paper and charcoal with the smooth skin of his body.

As she stroked and smudged the last few lines, she glanced over the edge of the paper and caught him watching her. She knew what he wanted as much as she.

To touch. Taste. Explore.

With one last stroke, she signed her name on the paper, claiming at least this image of him. She knew that to claim him in any other way would be substantially harder.

He was a man of intense emotion and passion, of great honor, and she wasn't sure she would measure up to his standards. But for this night, she intended to try.

Setting aside the pad and sketching materials, she stood. With trembling hands, she reached down, grabbed the hem of her nightshirt and, in one unbroken move, ripped it off her body.

Then she walked toward him.

Chapter 9

Ramona stopped within inches of him and did what she had been longing to do for so long. She laid her hand on the hollow above his heart, and the soft strands of his light-brown chest hair tickled her palm. Beneath that hair, his skin was cool to the touch.

"You're cold."

Unerringly, Diego covered her breast with his hand, his palm slightly rough.

"So are you."

The constant chill in her body came as a result of her system no longer producing the red blood cells it should. The lack of rest the last few days, combined with worry and excitement, had taxed her health to the brink. But she couldn't tell him that. Instead she said, "The loft's a big space and hard to heat at night."

A lie, Diego thought, sensing the quickening beat of her heart. But he wouldn't press her on it. Not now, when all he could think about was the touch of her hand on his skin, the feel of her hard nipple against his palm. Still, he wanted to make her comfortable. He stood and embraced her, using the powers of the demon to flood his body with heat and slowly spread to hers.

"You feel so good," she said, and pressed herself against him tighter. But when he noted the chill was gone from her flesh, he reined in the vampire, to maintain his human self.

As he held her, he said, "Tell me what you thought of as you sketched." He needed to know what was in her mind and possibly her heart.

She raised her hand, brushed back a lock of hair that had fallen forward onto his face. "I thought that this softened the line of your jaw."

Once she said it, she cupped his cheek and swept her thumb across his lips.

"What else?" he asked, intrigued by her almost hesitant touch.

She raised her other hand and laid it on the sharp ridge of his collarbone. Idly, she ran her fingers along that line and said, "I imagined how your skin would feel beneath my fingers. And you? What did you think of?"

He shocked himself by admitting, "How your mouth would feel against my nipple."

She brought her lips there, licked the edge of it with her tongue.

Her mouth was warm, wet. Amazing. He held her head to him, while he wrapped his other arm around her buttocks and brought her tight against his arousal. She pulled away, looked up at him. "What else did you think?"

His erection pressed against her belly, revealing what else he had desired. "I imagined you holding me, stroking me."

"Like this?" She snaked her hand downward and encircled him with her palm.

He watched, fascinated by the way her small hand enticed him toward satisfaction. So soft, but sure.

When she tongued his nipple again, he had to fight back his release.

She rose on tiptoe and kissed him, whispering against his lips, "It's okay to let go, Diego."

His breath exploded against her lips. "Not without you, *querida.*"

"Then touch me," she urged, and he brought his hand to her breast, where he caressed her nipple, until each pull of his hand created an answering tug between her legs.

"That's it, *amor.* Kiss me there," she pleaded as she continued to fondle him, each stroke slightly stronger, more insistent as her own passion rose.

He bent his head, took the hard tip into his mouth and sucked on its sweetness. He heard her soft cry of passion as he teethed the nipple.

She pressed her hips to his in invitation, and he accepted, plunging his hand downward to part her thighs. She was so wet and slick, he ached to feel her, taste her.

He dropped to his knees, forcing her to stop her ministrations, while he parted her with his fingers and unerringly found the center of her with his mouth. He sucked at the swollen bud of her clitoris and the smooth, wet lips protecting it. He slipped in first one finger and then a second, stroking and sucking her until her knees went weak.

He surged upward then, scooped her into his arms and carried her to the bed. He sat her on the edge and urged her to lie down as he positioned himself between her thighs, but didn't enter her. Instead, he lowered his head and kissed the pulse point at the base of her throat.

Ramona held his head to her and picked up her knees, cradling his hips. His erection brushed the curls between her legs. She wanted him inside of her, filling the emptiness caused by the desertion of his amazing hands and mouth. Reaching downward, she guided him to her, then stopped as reality reared up.

"I don't have protection," she whispered against the side of his face.

He raised his head, confused until her statement

finally registered. "I hadn't planned on this, either, but pleasure comes in many ways, *querida*."

As if to prove his point, he brought his hand down to where hers held his erection. He guided her hand away from him and to the entrance of her vagina, then joined her in caressing herself, urging her on. And as she slipped one finger inside, so did he.

"Diego," she said, tipping her head back and emitting a soft gasp as together they built her passion.

"*Así, amorcito*. Call my name when you come, *querida,*" he urged, and stroked faster until his fingers and hers were drenched and the beginning thrum of her climax arched her body up off the bed.

"*Ay,* Diego. *Amor,*" she called out, nearly overcome, but in sync with him as he moved, bringing his penis between her thighs.

Her hand slick with her own juices, she dragged it across the length of him, doing to him what he was doing to her. He felt it then—the rolling release that he craved.

He came, calling out her name as she breathed his in a cry of completion.

Her body warm from the bath they had shared to cleanse the remnants of their passion, Diego tucked her close to him, trying to contain that warmth. But it fled quickly.

Too quickly, he thought with concern.

Sneaking a peek at her, he noted the dark circles under her eyes, which seemed to be ever present lately. As she shivered and shifted near, he embraced her.

With a deep inhale, he once again sampled the scent of her, this time fresh from their bath. Their bodies were intertwined, allowing him to memorize the softness of her belly and thigh, the brush of her dark curls against his penis as it rested against her.

Despite his earlier satisfaction, he became aroused again, but forced desire back. Ramona needed to rest.

As she released a satisfied sigh and snuggled into his heat, contentment filled his heart, but so did sadness.

They had pleasured each other well, but he knew the physical satisfaction they had given one another wasn't enough. Yet he was wary of allowing it to go beyond that.

There was no such thing as a long-term relationship for him. Not with a human. Possibly not even with a vampire, he mused as he thought about Esperanza's untimely death, so sudden and without reason.

Maybe that was his punishment for his earlier decadent and selfish ways. Maybe that was why God had seen fit to doom him to a life of everlasting loss and uncontrollable change—to punish him for his past sins.

And Ramona? he thought, cradling her tighter as

she murmured his name in her sleep and a furrow marred her brow.

She was to be his for only an instant. Maybe only for this one pleasant night, since every moment with her was one filled with deceit.

His deceit about what he was. What he could give her, which was…

Nothing, Diego thought.

He closed his eyes and foolishly allowed himself to imagine he was human once again, with all the possibilities that could bring.

Ramona woke to the enticing smell of something sizzling on the stove. Cracking one eye open, she realized Diego was hard at work in her kitchen, cooking up a storm.

She lingered in bed, covertly watching him, imagining what it might be like to start every morning this way. But then reality intruded as her alarm sounded, not just to wake her. The annoyingly loud beeps were the call for her to head to the bathroom and down the assortment of pills necessary to keep her failing body running.

At the sound of the alarm, Diego raised his head and beamed her a smile. It caused a painful constriction in her heart, but she forced an answering smile and, wrapping the sheet around her, walked to where he stood at her stove.

Rising on tiptoe, she brushed a kiss on his lips, but he was not appeased with that simple peck.

He wrapped an arm around her waist, drawing her up so he could open his mouth against hers and entice her to answer his demand by slipping her tongue into his mouth. She kissed him deeply, uncaring of anything except how good it felt to begin the morning like this, next to him.

When they broke apart, she was breathless and holding on to his shoulders for support. As she met his gaze, she noted his worry.

"You still look tired. Maybe you should have shut off your alarm and gotten more rest."

"I'll take a nap later." She turned from him, intent on taking her medicines before she ate, but he asked, "Where are you going?"

"Morning breath," she said as an excuse, then she hurried to the bathroom, where she pulled out the half-dozen prescription bottles from her medicine chest. With a sip of water, she took her dosage, no longer caring which was to boost her hematocrit or keep at bay the painful headaches that sometimes attacked when she least expected.

Taking a breath, she leaned her hands on the sink and waited, hoping her stomach would keep the medications down this morning. Some mornings she was not so lucky.

Today was a good day, she thought.

She took a moment to brush her teeth and comb her hair. A quick splash of cold water against her face revived her. For good measure, she pinched her cheeks, thinking that with a hint of color, she might not draw Diego's concerned attention again.

When she exited the bathroom, he had already set the table and was placing plates piled high with food before the two chairs. He gestured for her to take a place, and she slipped into the seat, inhaled the enticing aromas of bacon, eggs and toast. When he put a mug of coffee before her, she moaned, "I think I'm in heaven."

He smiled and slipped into the seat beside her. With a wink, he said, "If I had known this was all it takes to make you happy, we could have skipped last night."

"*Amor,* I wouldn't have skipped last night for the world," she said, and laid her hand on his as it rested on the table.

He twined his fingers with hers. "Me, neither. Eat up. I have to get going and make some calls."

"What do you hope to find out?" she asked as she forked up some eggs.

"Which appraisers looked at the paintings. How the paintings got to the auction house and then to the buyers. I may even pay Alicia a call, if you'd like to come?" He watched as Ramona ate, but left his own plate untouched.

"I'd like to come with you if it won't seem odd." She gestured with her fork to his food. "Please eat. There's nothing worse than cold eggs."

Diego did as she had requested. He ate just to maintain the semblance of being human. Only blood could provide any real sustenance. He recalled things far worse than this meal, such as the mealy bread and worm-filled meat they'd fed him in his cell during the Inquisition. Or the chilling blood of one of his dead companions on the first trip he and Esperanza had made out west. They had been trapped in a mountain snowstorm, and to avoid feeding on the living, they had drained the dead to keep alive.

After a few forkfuls, he said, "Alicia bought the largest painting." The one he had hoped to keep himself, he mused regretfully, but then continued, "We're supposed to deliver it in a few days, and you could come along to help hang it."

Not an unusual occurrence in the art world. Some buyers even paid extra for the artist to come and assure that the work was properly displayed.

"Do you think she'll let us look at the painting she bought from van Winter?" Ramona asked.

"The question isn't whether we'll be able to see it. Alicia keeps most of her paintings in one special room. Her own museum of sorts, complete with a sophisticated security system."

"You've been there, obviously. So, once we see it, I'll know if it's the painting I did." Ramona laid down her fork, no doubt filled with anticipation.

Diego noticed the early morning light creep over the edge of one of Ramona's skylights and realized he couldn't linger for much longer. Although his age allowed him a little immunity from the effects of sunlight, too much would weaken him. Full midafternoon sun for an extended period of time could kill him.

He suspected he would need all his strength in the days to come, until they had a better handle on what van Winter had done, or what the recluse would do if he suspected Ramona was trying to expose his deceit. Diego also needed to keep his wits about him regarding Ramona, reminding himself of both her humanity and her beauty. Beautiful packages sometimes hid ugly contents.

"Once we know for sure, we'll have to prove it somehow," he said, and rose from the table.

"My paints contain titanium. Polarized-light microscopy will show that, but it's not likely Ms. Tipton will let us take a sample, right?"

Diego shook his head. "If she did, are you prepared to go to jail for forgery?"

Chapter 10

Some might call her a fool, but she definitely had not intended to help van Winter deceive anyone.

"I made copies, Diego. Not forgeries. Being in the art world, you should know the difference."

"Did you sign them with the artists' names?" he challenged, and she wondered why he hadn't asked this and a host of other questions before now. Possibly because they had been too busy doing things they maybe shouldn't have been doing.

"I didn't, but the names were on the paintings at the gallery. It surprised me to see them there," she admitted. "I didn't use older canvases or stretcher frames. They were brand-new."

"The appraisers would have checked those items

for age," Diego said as he paced back and forth. Then he paused and faced her. "But if van Winter went so far as to add the signatures, maybe he altered that, as well."

"Or maybe he replaced mine with the originals from the paintings. The frames looked old when I examined them in the gallery. Removing them would alter the value of the real pieces, but help him carry out the fraud with the copies."

"Someone should have noticed an exchange like that. The nail holes and mounting marks should have tipped them off."

"Unless the appraisers didn't carefully check. The provenance of the works is faultless. The van Winter family was known to have been in possession of the paintings for quite some time," Ramona said, running through all the things she might examine if she were in the role of authenticating the works.

Diego picked up where she left off. "The craquelure would be off."

Ramona winced as she thought of the care she had used to replicate the fine cracks and lines due to the age of the paintings. As Diego noticed her response, he sighed. "I'm guessing you're as good at that as you are at painting."

"I guess, but if someone took the time to do a full Morellian analysis—"

"I know one of the owners of that auction house and suspect that his interest in the commission may be greater than his concern for the authenticity of the works."

A ray of light inched onto the tabletop as the sun rose higher in the morning sky. Diego shifted away from it as he said, "It's getting late. If I'm going to reach out to some of my contacts, I need to go."

Ramona had things of her own to do that day, most importantly, a visit to her hematologist to discuss the results of the blood tests she'd had earlier in the week. She walked Diego to the door, where she stood before him uncertainly, not quite sure where things stood after their passionate night but rather businesslike morning.

"Will I see you later?" she asked, waiting awkwardly.

He slipped on his suit jacket, and when he noticed her apprehension, kissed her cheek. "I'll be by, but first I want to get some things straight."

She suspected it was about more than just the paintings, but still needed to hear it from him. "About the forgeries?"

His hand dropped heavily and he fiddled with straightening his jacket. With a sigh, he finally answered, "About that and more. Whatever this is between us...I need to think about it. Think about the consequences."

"Right." After she closed the door behind him, she realized she should be thankful that someone in this relationship—if that's what it was—was thinking with his head.

Maybe it was time she gave it more thought, too, reminding herself that she wasn't someone to pin hopes on for a long-term relationship.

While she prayed the doctor would give her some reason for optimism, in her heart she feared the prognosis would be worse.

Your heart didn't lie to you about some things.

Diego ran his hands over the frame, hesitant about the course of action he had decided on. For over four centuries, he had possessed this painting and a few others, holding on to them as a last connection with his past and a safeguard for his future. If he needed to sell them, they would fetch quite a tidy sum.

Luckily, his business sense and other investments made it unnecessary to go to such extremes.

But now his association with Ramona required that he reveal the existence of this painting.

Ramona. In the many years he had known her, she had always brought a bright spot to his life and, although he wouldn't admit it, to his heart. Last night had been…

Extraordinary. Overwhelming. Dangerous.

He couldn't allow himself to forget what he was. What he could not possess—a human.

Unlike the painting in his hands, Ramona could never be his.

"Diego? What are you doing?" Simon asked as he limped over, leaning heavily on his walking sticks.

"Just wondering about…things." He caressed

the frame, its edges sharp beneath his fingers. Cold. Lifeless.

"You came in rather late this morning," Simon noted as he dropped into the chair beside him, leaned over and examined what Diego held in his hands. "Quite beautiful," his keeper said.

"Yes. Quite," he agreed, although his mind wasn't on the painting.

Simon must have sensed it, for he said, "She must be special."

Diego looked up and examined his keeper's wizened countenance. The man had aged greatly in the past few weeks without the special bite Diego had been bestowing during the last century. Despite the aging and the death it would soon bring, peace filled Simon's face.

The last time Diego had felt peace like that had been…last night in Ramona's arms. After the sex, as he'd lain there, holding her and watching her sleep, he'd felt peace. Until she had turned in his arms and he'd noticed the small smudges along her thighs. His fingerprints marking her. Reminding him of her fragility.

Of her mortality.

"I need to go," he said and finished wrapping the painting in the centuries-old canvas. He tucked the picture into the padded crate he had brought home from the gallery.

When he walked to the door, Simon called out to him, "Diego, it's not all bad, you know."

"What isn't all bad?" he asked, confused by his keeper's comment.

"The living beyond your time. When you have the right people with you, it's not so bad."

An aura of vitality swirled around Ramona when she rolled open the door to her apartment. In addition to that increased hum of energy, a becoming flush tinged her cheeks and her smile brightened her eyes.

When Diego stepped inside, she stood before him hesitantly, wiping her hands on the apron she wore. The sweet aroma of tomato sauce spiced the air, and he gave an appreciative sniff, as he expected a human date might.

"Smells good." He laid a hand at her waist and drew her close. She met him for a kiss and after, with a smile on his face, he said, "Tastes better."

Ramona shot him a tentative smile and slipped her hand into his. "I thought the least I could do was make dinner to thank you."

He followed her to the kitchen table, where he held up the bundle of mail he'd picked up on his way in.

Ramona motioned to the island. "Just leave it there. I'll look at it later."

Seeing her busy at the stove, her back to him, he asked, "Can I help with anything?"

"Why don't you open the wine."

He did as she asked, then poured two glasses of

merlot and took them over to her. With her free hand, she accepted a glass and raised it to his. "*Salud, amor y pesetas.*"

He smiled at her use of the Spanish toast, and sipped the wine. Full-bodied and earthy, the merlot was a welcome change on his palate from his usual beverage—blood. "Very nice," he murmured. She shrugged. "I'm sure you're used to a better vintage. And much fancier cuisine."

"Without the company, even the finest meal would seem bland."

Ramona chuckled. "Smooth, Diego. Does that work with all the women?"

Her comment awakened him to her ambivalence. "I sense you have an issue with my charm. Or is it about my wealth?"

She put the cover back on the sauce and faced him. "So you admit you are quite well-off?"

"Quite. Is that an issue?" he pressed as she walked past him to set the table.

He stepped around and grabbed hold of her hand. "You're pushing me away today. Why?" But even as he asked the question, he realized that maybe it was for the best. They were just too different in ways that could never be harmonized.

Ramona looked down at their hands and twined her fingers through his as she said, "Last night…it was great. Duh, as if you didn't already know that."

He gave a playful shake of their hands. "Definitely amazing, but too fast. I really want to know more about you. Let things develop a little more slowly."

"You can't rush a fine wine," she quipped. Though fearing what she might see, she risked a glance at him, and felt relieved at the caring she noted on his features. Would it turn to pity if he knew she didn't have the time to let things develop more slowly? That she had to grab life and everything in it quickly, before it disappeared?

And yet she knew he was right. She'd known it even as they had satisfied each other last night. "So, tonight is about..."

"Getting to know each other." He bent and kissed her, a soft, gentle kiss nothing like those from the night before.

When they broke apart, he smiled and said, "So how was your day?"

Guilt twisted in her belly, because everything she said now would be a lie. "I went back to sleep. Then I got up and did some work."

She moved away from him, worried that he would pick up on her deception, and busied herself with serving dinner as he sat down at the table.

"How was *your* day?" she asked, eager to move the focus from herself.

Diego began an account of what he had done earlier. "I spoke to Richard Bridge from the auction house, and he provided me with the name of the appraiser."

"And...?" Ramona brought the plates over and placed one before Diego.

After taking a forkful of pasta, he continued. "Knowing him as I do, I worried that he might not have taken adequate care about the provenance of the works, but the appraiser he hired had impressive credentials."

"You were able to speak with the appraiser today?" she asked.

"He was more than eager to come see the painting I claimed to have."

"Claimed to have?"

Diego paused with his fork halfway to his mouth. "El Greco. An oil from his days in Toledo."

Her own fork clattered to her plate. "El Greco?" she squeaked, well aware of the price a painting by that master would bring.

Diego sensed her surprise and discomfort. She was already hung up about the differences in their financial situations, so to calm her concerns, he lied. "I had access to the painting, and I must say that Williams, the appraiser, did exactly what I would expect a competent appraiser to do."

"He authenticated the painting just like that?" She snapped her fingers for emphasis.

"Actually, no. He made notes of several details, including the fact that it wasn't in its original frame. He indicated he wanted to do some additional analysis, much as he should, since the work was one previously uncataloged anywhere."

"An El Greco that no one has seen before? How unusual. But if the provenance was in order—"

"I told Mr. Williams I needed help with the provenance."

Silence followed his statement. After a long pause, Ramona said, "You asked him to help you fake the paperwork?"

He shrugged. "Not in so many words, but yes, I guess that's what I was implying."

When he hesitated, Ramona urged him on with a wave of her hand. "And he said—?"

"Good day and here's my bill. I believed him. So we're back to square one, because it doesn't seem as if the auction house or the appraiser was in on whatever switch happened."

Ramona peered into her wineglass and swirled the contents around before stating, "You said yesterday that you wouldn't put it past your friend to not care about the authenticity."

"But I also know that Richard's the kind of man who can't help bragging. If he had pulled off something like this, he couldn't keep from letting me know." At his words Ramona slumped in her chair, some of her earlier animation gone. Diego laid a hand on her shoulder and said, "We'll figure this out."

She nodded, sipped her wine and motioned to his half-eaten plate. "Did you like it?"

He had. Normally he ate human food only to keep up appearances, and didn't much care how it tasted. But the sauce had been particularly good and the small amount of garlic had barely registered with his vamp physique.

"It's very good," he said, and in an effort to please her, he ate some more.

Ramona tackled her own plate, her appetite surprisingly good today. Maybe it had been the earlier transfusion that her physician, Melissa Danvers, had insisted on after her poor lab results. The transfusion had given Ramona more energy than she'd had in weeks. She wanted to make the most of how she felt today....

Including making the most of the time she was spending with Diego, since based on the lab results, her time might be growing short.

Because she didn't want to keep on discussing her problems with van Winter, she turned the conversation toward the painting she had started earlier that afternoon—an oil of the sketch she had made of Diego the night before. It would take some time for her to really do it justice.

Time she would fight for, she decided. The painting had become about something more. About hanging on long enough to explore the emotion growing in her heart. Maybe even about hoping that she would get better and be able to grow old with this man who intrigued her so.

When they finished the meal, she started clearing the table and rinsing plates for the dishwasher when Diego said, "Let me do it. That's the least I can do to help."

She wanted to argue that he had done quite a lot to help her already, but she saw the earnest look on his face. Maybe a little touch of the common man's world was a novelty to him, she thought. She suspected that Diego rarely did dishes.

With a nod, she left him to the cleaning up, taking a seat at the kitchen table and finishing her wine as she observed him. Contrary to what she might have thought, he was quite proficient—and a totally arresting sight as he stood at her sink.

He had dressed casually tonight, but that did nothing to take away from his inherent grace and elegance. The stylish jeans he wore hung loosely on his lean hips and long legs, but the simple black knit Henley hugged every muscle in his chest and arms.

Heat rose up in her as she remembered those arms around her. The press of his chest as he'd held her.

She finished her wine and poured another little bit from the bottle. While a glass a day helped with her low iron count, anything more was out of the question with all the medications she was taking. As she sipped that final portion, she noted the mail Diego had dropped on the island earlier.

Glass in hand, she walked over and undid the rubber band the postman had slipped around the bundle. She tossed aside the usual junk mail and bills, but paused as she got to the big white envelope that had been wrapped around the other mail. Placing her glass of wine down, she opened it and peered inside.

Photos? she wondered, reaching in and removing them.

As she saw what they were, she gasped in shock.

Chapter 11

Diego had just placed the last plate in the dishwasher when he heard Ramona's stunned gasp. Turning, he noted that all color had fled from her face and that her hands shook as she picked up some papers from the island. He went to her and gently guided her to a chair since she didn't look very steady.

He took from her what he realized were photos. The first image gave him no cause for alarm. Just a mundane multistory brick building on some nicely kept grounds. The next photo troubled him more. An older woman with a strong resemblance to Ramona sat in a chair, staring blankly out through sliding glass doors. Beside her, a young candy striper read from a magazine.

"Your mother?"

With a trembling bob of her head, Ramona explained. "After van Winter's first threat, I moved her to a different nursing home."

From Ramona's reaction, Diego guessed these photos were from the new location.

Careful not to handle them any more than was necessary, he slipped them back into the envelope. "I have a friend who can help us."

"Van Winter warned me—"

"She's with the FBI. She can be trusted." He stroked Ramona's back with a soothing gesture, but the tension in her muscles remained.

"Why would she want to help me?" Ramona faced him, determination etched into her features as if to say that no matter what, she could take care of herself.

He cradled her cheek. "Because she's my friend and because I care about you."

FBI agents clearly didn't keep regular hours, Ramona thought as she and Diego entered the club where they had agreed to meet his friends. Still nervous about expanding the circle of people aware of van Winter's actions and her own involvement in the fraud, she nevertheless knew she had to trust others if she was going to protect her mother. More than anything, that was the one thing that concerned her.

That and making sure Diego stayed safe, as well,

she thought when they walked through the crowded club barely an hour later.

As they approached the bar, the neon sign for the Lair gleamed bright red, spewing light onto the customers and seeming to spill blood onto the gleaming stainless surface. It reminded her of her one visit to the morgue, part of a tough-love session at juvie. The administrators had figured it best to show the detainees where they might end up if they didn't mend their ways.

Well, she had changed her path in life, but still found herself with an express ticket to the same destination.

"You okay?" Diego asked, leaning toward her to combat the noise from the rock band loudly playing onstage.

"Fine," she said, although a knot had formed in her stomach after they had left her apartment for this rendezvous.

Evidently spotting his friends, Diego waved to a man and woman seated at the bar.

The man was starkly handsome, with dark hair and a goatee that framed a mouth that should be declared illegal. As his eyes roved over Ramona, assessing, she realized how dark and fathomless they appeared, until the slim woman next to him laid a hand on his thigh. Life filled him with that touch, somehow lessening the severity of his appearance.

Ramona examined the woman, the FBI agent. For a chauvinistic moment she wondered how such a small person could possibly stop one of van Winter's steroid-amplified goons, but as their gazes locked from across the distance, Ramona discerned the woman was not to be taken lightly. Steely determination filled her otherwise tired-looking face.

When the two of them stopped before the couple, the woman rose. "Let's go to the office, where it'll be more private."

Without waiting, she walked off, and the threesome followed her, weaving through the crowd and up some narrow stairs.

The staircase was so tight and airless that Ramona experienced a moment of claustrophobia before reaching a more spacious hallway on the next floor. From there, it was just a few short steps to the office, a nice-size room filled with touches of old-world charm totally at odds with the shlocky vampire-themed space below.

Once inside, the petite woman turned and finally introduced herself. "Special Agent Diana Reyes," she said, and offered her hand.

Ramona shook it. "Ramona Escobar."

Diana's companion spoke next. "Ryder Latimer. I own this place."

Which made her wonder why he was trustworthy with her mother's life. But if Diego had faith in him, Ramona would honor that confidence. "Thank you for agreeing to help me."

"Any friend of Diego's is our friend, as well," Ryder said, although his tone seemed to be dubious of the "friendship" claim. Quite frankly, he was spot on. She and Diego weren't just friends. Of course, they weren't lovers, either, in the true sense of the word.

They had had sex. Where that put them on the relationship scale she didn't know.

Diego coughed uncomfortably as if warning Ryder to go no further with that statement. Instead, he took command, motioning that they should all sit down on the couch and chairs at one side of Ryder's office. After, he filled in Diana and Ryder on all that had happened, and the information he had been able to get earlier that day.

Diana listened patiently, her green, catlike eyes shifting from Ramona to Diego, clearly assessing everything. Her skin was pale despite its slightly olive cast, or maybe it appeared pale because of her dark, nearly seal-black hair, closely cropped at the nape, but longer up top. Her serviceable white shirt coupled with the dark suit seemed to indicate that she had come straight from work. As Ramona took a closer look, she noted the edge of a black leather shoulder strap when Diana leaned forward and braced her elbows on her knees. A quick peek confirmed a telltale bulge near her left armpit.

The woman was lethally armed, and not just physically, Ramona decided. She had a competent but dangerous air about her, warning that she was not to be messed with. Her questions confirmed that impression.

"So there's no one who can corroborate the threats?" she asked, leaning back into the wing chair stationed across from where Diego and Ramona sat on the couch.

"He chased everyone out of the room before he cornered me in the gallery."

Looking to Diego, Diana said, "You didn't see or hear a specific threat."

"I saw the aftermath," he replied with some annoyance, but Ramona laid a hand on his arm.

"It's okay if she doesn't believe me. Sometimes I'm not sure this is all real myself."

"It's not that I don't believe you, Ramona," Diana replied. "But if I have to take this to someone else, I need enough information for them to believe me. I don't have that right now."

"No, you don't," she agreed. "But maybe this will help." She passed Diana the envelope and photos she had received in the mail. Before coming over, Diego had slipped them into a reclosable plastic bag, hoping to preserve whatever fingerprint evidence might be on the materials.

Diana nodded. "This may help, but let's go over everything step-by-step."

Ramona did as she requested, describing every meeting she could think of and every aspect of her relationship with van Winter save one—the terminal illness that had most likely been the reason he had chosen her for his deception.

When Diana questioned her about the money

van Winter had paid her and why she hadn't suspected his true intent, Ramona admitted that her main concern had been her mother's welfare. Time and time again Diana pressed, trying to elicit one fact or another, and Ramona answered as best she could.

It seemed forever before the agent turned her attention to Diego once again, and by then Ramona had a fierce headache. She rubbed at her temples, grimacing as the pain grew in intensity. She closed her eyes for just a moment, hoping it would pass, but it remained.

When she opened her eyes, she noticed that both Ryder and Diego were staring at her. She felt liquid heat trickling from her nose. Swiping at it, her fingers came away wet with bright red blood.

She pinched her nose and tilted her head back, thinking that this was so wrong. She had taken the new medicines Melissa had prescribed, and she'd been feeling so much better after the transfusion in the early afternoon.

A second later, Diana was kneeling beside her on the couch and pressing ice wrapped in a wet towel against her forehead.

The towel hampered her sight, but Ramona sensed that Ryder and Diego were no longer in the room. "Diego…"

"I asked the men to get us some more ice," Diana explained, but Ramona sensed the FBI agent was being less than truthful.

A moment later, she felt the sweep of Diana's hand, pushing the sleeve of her sweater upward to reveal the transfusion marks on her arm. Ramona reacted quickly, brushing her hand away and pulling the sleeve back into place. The damage had been done, however.

With another towel, Diana dabbed at her nostrils, cleaning away the blood there, and little by little, the nosebleed receded and the headache lessened to a bearable ache.

"Why don't we get you cleaned up before the guys come back?" Diana rose and pointed to a door on the far side of the room. "Ryder's private bathroom."

Ramona followed her there and, once inside, washed her face and hands.

Diana stood in the doorway, blocking the exit, her arms crossed over her middle. "Those tracks on your arm are pretty extreme. I don't think you're a major-league junkie, so what's the deal?"

Ramona knew there was no use lying. "I've got a rare form of anemia. The marks are from the tests and transfusions."

Diana was blunt and to the point. "Must be pretty serious."

Ramona decided to be just as straightforward. "Deadly serious. I'm dying."

Up until now Diana had been all-business. But now compassion softened her eyes. "You haven't told him, have you?"

"Will you?" Ramona challenged, afraid of all the complications the revelation would bring. Afraid that once Diego knew, she would never be able to explore the emotions that had been developing between them.

Diana vacillated, then cursed beneath her breath and stalked away. She paced, her shoes squeaking on the tiled floor, before she faced her once again. "He's my friend. I can't lie to him."

"I'm not asking you to lie. I just need a little time."

As before, Diana seemed conflicted. She finally relented, but not before making a demand. "Call your doctor. I get the sense this nosebleed wasn't a good thing." She handed Ramona her cell phone.

Ramona wasn't about to argue, because Diana was right. Dialing Melissa's number, she hit Send, and was surprised to see Diana's phone indicate there was a match with her contacts list.

"You know Melissa Danvers?" she asked.

"She's my sister-in-law," Diana replied. "And a good doctor. I'll give you some privacy." With that, she left the room.

Melissa answered with a cheerful, "*Hola,* sister-in-law. What's up?"

"Actually, it's Ramona Escobar." She hesitated, sure that Melissa had to be wondering why she was on Diana's phone, but then plowed forward. "My cell phone died."

"Something's wrong?" Melissa asked, shifting from friend to doctor mode.

"Whopper of a headache followed by a small nosebleed."

From close to the mouthpiece came the sounds of a baby starting to fuss. Melissa gently cooed to her daughter and called out to her husband. Ramona said, "Listen, I'm fine now."

"I'm going to recheck the earlier blood tests, and maybe we should run some more. Can you come by tomorrow morning so I can take another look at you?"

"Sure." What else did she have to do besides avoiding van Winter, working on her final painting and hiding the truth from Diego?

Chapter 12

Diego held Ramona's hand as they walked down the stairs, leaving Diana and Ryder in the office. Down below, in the main area of the club, a different band had taken the stage and the lights had been dimmed, creating a darker and infinitely more intimate atmosphere. One that he decided not to waste.

"How are you feeling?" He peered down at her, and even in the shadowy light, a flush of color was evident on her cheeks. Her hands, however, were chilled.

"I'm feeling better. Care to dance?" she asked, preempting him by posing the question.

"I'd love to."

He twined his fingers with hers and eased near, but it wasn't enough. Not nearly enough. He wrapped one arm around her waist, closing the distance between them.

She slipped her arms to his back, urging him tight, and swayed with him to the insinuating beat of the bass. Diego focused on the beat of her heart.

He bent his head and inhaled her scent, fresh and clean, but with the faint remnant of blood. The sight of it, bright and red on her skin from the nosebleed, had driven him and Ryder from the room before their demons had emerged enough to be noticed.

The demon within him fixated on that faint scent now, but Diego chased the vampire away, wanting just one thing for this night. To be human.

He allowed himself to revel in the press of her body, so slight against his greater size, and in the soft curves shaping themselves to his hardness. He wanted to sink into all that softness and lose himself in her humanity.

In the dark intimacy of the crowd, he reached between their bodies and cradled her breast, caressing it until her nipple pebbled to life beneath his fingers. He found the tip and caressed it, delighting in the murmured moan that slipped from her lips and the way her fingers dug into the muscles of his back.

With small steps, he gradually inched them off the dance floor to the edge of the room, where it was darker, and found an outcropping in the fake stone wall. He eased them behind it, providing a smidgen of privacy, which he seized, slipping his hand under her sweater.

She was naked beneath the fabric.

Finding her skin smooth and slightly damp, he inched his hand up until her tight nipple nestled against his palm. She moaned once again and he stroked his thumb back and forth across the tip until she brought her hand up and covered his.

"Can we go home? I don't want it to be here," she whispered against his lips.

"What don't you want to be here?" he asked, dropping a kiss at the side of her mouth even as he caressed her breast again.

"The first time we truly make love."

As they rushed to her apartment, he actually wished that Ramona knew he was a vampire. He could have used his supernatural speed to get back instead of hailing a cab and battling the traffic.

Somehow he kept his hands from wandering during the short ride up to her loft, not wishing to press. He wanted to let things move slowly so that when they did make love, there would be no doubt on either of their parts.

His inner voice warned that there wasn't enough time to eliminate all the doubts he felt, but he shoved that voice away. His vampire self had nothing to do with what was about to happen, since he refused to allow the demon to interfere tonight. He wanted to be human for Ramona. He wanted her to experience all that a man and woman should when they cared for each other.

The demon within him knew nothing of that. It knew only about the call of the blood in her veins and the sex that roused it to violence.

When they reached her loft, he helped her roll open the door. They barely managed to close it before they went into each other's arms.

The urgency that hadn't left him since the Lair redoubled, but he tempered his need. Ramona wasn't the kind of woman who did this lightly. He wanted it to be special for her.

He wanted, for this night, to forget that forever wasn't possible for them because of what he was and would forever be. He wanted to forget that the woman in his arms had secrets.

The shudder that racked Diego's body warned Ramona of the insanity of continuing. She could never give him any of the things a man wanted. Time would not allow her that.

Selfish as it was, however, she also didn't want this night to end. If she could somehow stop time, this was where she would pause the moment for eternity.

Risking a peek at him, she noted his indecision, but also the carefully banked need as he brushed his lips against hers and said, "I can't promise anything."

"Neither can I."

Those words released his restraint, and he opened his mouth, deepened the kiss. She accepted him, welcoming the thrust of his tongue and the promise of his arms as he tightened his hold on her.

She met the dance of his tongue with hers, and tasted him. Memorized the crush of his hard body, so big and strong compared to hers. Her breath ragged against his lips, she pressed herself to him.

He answered by sweeping one arm beneath her knees and lifting her off the floor. With a whirl, he carried her to her bed at the far end of the loft. He set her down beside the four-poster, and then sat on the edge. Denied the loving crush of his body, she protested, until he smiled at her, grasped her upper arms and urged her into the vee of his widespread legs. His intent became clear then. She reached down and, with trembling hands, pulled her sweater up and over her head, exposing herself.

He cupped her breasts and strummed his thumbs across her nipples, beading them into pebbly points. She moaned and laid her hands on his shoulders as her knees grew weak.

His ice-blue eyes had darkened with desire when he finally looked up. "You're so beautiful," he said, before he put his mouth to one breast and tenderly sucked the tip.

Between her legs, the pulse of her desire thickened and grew into needy throbs with each pull of his mouth and tweak of his fingers. Unsteady, she wrapped one arm around his shoulders while she cradled his head, her fingers tunneling into the long strands of his thick hair. She urged him on with soft cries.

"Shh, *amor,*" Diego whispered against her breast, and as he had before, he lifted her, reversing their positions on the bed so that she was now the one sitting on the edge and he was the supplicant before her, begging for her touch.

She didn't disappoint him, quickly yanking off the knit Henley to reveal his upper body and run her hands along the muscles of his abdomen. She pressed her mouth to the center of his torso and tongued the ridge of muscle there, then rose off the bed to allow her mouth and tongue access to his chest.

She slipped her lips over a nipple, tugging and sucking on it, and he shuddered, loving the feel of her mouth and hands on him and the way her breasts brushed his body as she sought to please him. His erection throbbed, needing attention.

"Touch me," he said, urging her hand downward until it cupped him through the soft fabric of his jeans.

It wasn't enough for him. She must have sensed it, for she sat back on the edge of the bed and with trembling hands undid his snap and zipper, tugging down his pants. She encircled him with one hand and stroked him, the pull of her hand drawing a shaky breath from him.

Heavy-lidded and sensuous, her dark brown eyes were nearly black with passion as she asked, "Can I kiss you here?"

"*Por favor,*" he groaned. She bent, brushed the faintest kiss across the tip, but it was enough to make him jump in her hand. A sexy half smile came to her lips before she completed the kiss, sucking the tip of him into her mouth while she caressed him with her hands.

He closed his eyes for a moment, the sight of her going down on him almost too much to bear. Excitement and desire rose faster than he'd imagined possible, awakening the demon in him. It knew what would normally come next.

The shock of that realization jolted Diego.

Ramona wasn't like the others. She was special, and he needed to show her that.

Easing away from her caress, he kicked off his jeans and briefs before returning to where she sat, a puzzled look on her face. He eased her confusion by saying, "I want this to be about us together."

He urged her to lie down on the bed so that he could remove her jeans. She was naked beneath them and his body grew heavy at the thought of sliding into her, but he battled back that image, not wanting to rush.

He met her gaze and held out his hand. "Come with me." He knelt on the bed, shifted until he was in the middle and she was beside him. Slowly he eased them down onto the sheet until they were lying side by side, their bodies brushing against each other.

Tenderly he reached up and cradled her face in his hands. He hesitated, wanting to tell her how much this meant to him, but words failed him, so instead, he kissed her. The kiss was delicate and inviting, urging her to join him.

She answered, moving perfectly in sync with him. When he lifted one hand to her breast, she followed, tracing the edge of his nipple with her finger. She slipped her hand downward to caress him, and he lowered his hand between her legs, parting her to find her center.

Ramona sucked in a ragged breath as he eased one finger inside her. Raising her thigh, she slipped it over his, providing him greater access. He accepted her invitation, easing yet another finger deep within, mimicking what he would do later with his body.

He felt her, wet and hot. And he wanted it, too.

She shifted to her back and guided him to her. As she looked up at him, she noticed the tight lines of his body, the restraint he had been showing up until now, and said, "Release yourself."

Diego's arms shook as he poised above her, the tip of him at the moist entrance of her womb. Her words reverberated through his skull, awakening the darkness within him, rousing the beast who normally emerged for such diversions.

Shaking his head, he forced back the vampire, wanting his human self to experience the delights of her body and the comfort of the arms she wrapped around him. "Come with me, *amor*."

She reached to the nightstand, dragged out a small packet and with a speed that surprised him, opened it and eased the condom over him, tenderly stroking even as she positioned him between her legs.

He slipped inside her tightness, overwhelmed not just by the sensation of her warm, willing body accepting his, but by the tenderness of her kiss against his brow and the loving caress of her hand across his face before she sank back down onto the mattress and met his gaze.

He saw it then. The love he had never expected to see again in his eternal life. The promise of so much more than just the physical release their bodies craved. The emotion was so strong it nearly undid him, and so he closed his eyes, focusing on the union of their bodies.

He moved tentatively at first, acclimating himself to feel her beneath him, the tightness around him, slick with the passion he had earlier aroused.

She whispered his name, an entreaty to take her further, and he pushed, increasing the strength of his thrusts until their breathing rasped in the quiet night. Her knees came up around him, and her hands held tight to his shoulders.

He needed more. He needed to taste her, and so he bent his head and suckled one breast, dragging a moan from her.

She held his head to her and arched her back, giving him greater access.

He felt it then, the beginning tremors of her climax rising from deep within her body, calling to his to answer. He gave himself over to the sensations of loving her: her skin, smooth and supple as his abdomen grazed hers; the hard tips of her breasts against his chest.

The smell of her arousal and of the blood surging through her body.

The beast protested then, clawing to be set free, but Diego battled the vampire back as he had earlier, and thrust into her again and again until her body climaxed beneath his and she cried out his name.

Her muscles pulsed around him as he stroked yet again, searching for his own release. When she lifted upward and tongued his nipple, his body jerked with pleasure and it began then, pooling at his center and moving outward.

Heat. Strong, demanding heat. Uncontrollable desire.

He bent his head, the vampire beginning to assert control as the strength of their passion drove back the human, who had not experienced such joy in centuries. As Diego buried his head in the crook between her neck and shoulder, her pulse beat madly against the vamp-sensitized skin of his lips.

The blood called to him and Diego lost it.

The demon erupted even as he savored the release of his body.

He reared away from her, trying to rein in the vampire, which wanted nothing more than to sink his long, lethal fangs into her neck, but it was too late.

She had seen his true face and recoiled, scrambling away from him as he knelt before her on the bed.

He held out his hands in a pleading gesture. "Forgive me."

"What are you?" she asked, hands crossed against her chest to hide her nakedness.

"I'm a vampire."

Ramona shook her head in disbelief. "A vampire? An honest-to-goodness blood-sucking vampire?"

No answer was necessary. The proof was there, right before her in the strange blue-green gleam of his eyes and the bright white fangs that reached nearly to the middle of his chin.

Despite that, she shook her head and closed her eyes, as if the image might somehow change. But when she opened them once more, the demon remained, only this time he was fully clothed. In Diego's clothing. His own clothes, she reminded herself, realizing that the creature before her *was* Diego. Her Diego.

"How did you do that?" she asked, motioning awkwardly.

"Vamp speed."

Vamp speed. So calmly stated, as if he hadn't just upended their entire world with his revelation.

"Ramona," he said, and moved toward her, slowly morphing back to human as he did so.

"Get out," she said, and pointed to the door, alternately confused and guilty about all that had just happened.

"*Por favor.* Let me explain," he pleaded, something she suspected he wasn't used to doing.

Diego Rivera didn't plead or ask or beg. He took. She had known that much about him from the get-go, and his actions tonight just proved it. But her own conscience pricked at her, reminding her that he hadn't been the only who hadn't been truthful.

As her fear and outrage ebbed with that realization, she found the strength to make her own confession.

"No, let *me* explain. I'm dying," she stated simply.

"All humans die," he responded, and dragged a hand through his locks, still in disarray from her hands.

She already missed the feel of them sliding through her fingers, but forced herself to make her statement clearer. "I'm terminally ill. I may not survive the autumn, Diego. I didn't mean for this—"

He was on her, grabbing her arms and shaking so hard her teeth rattled together. "What do you mean?"

"Van Winter called me a dead woman walking, and he was right. It was probably why he chose me for his scheme."

Diego's hands dropped from her arms and his eyes slowly bled out, becoming the strange neon blue-green of the vampire. Fangs inched downward, but he retracted them, clearly fighting for control. When he finally spoke, an odd rumble tinged his voice, like that of a big jungle cat.

"You lied to me. Did you lie about everything else?"

She wanted to alleviate his doubts, wanted him to believe in her, but maybe this was for the best. They had lied to each other about things that were too important. Nothing could ever come of a relationship based on such lies.

He was a vampire and she was…

As good as dead.

Chapter 13

Not even vamp speed was enough to outrun Ramona's last words: "I don't ever want to see you again."

He leaped to the roof of her building and hurried away, trying to escape the look of betrayal on her face. Still, even with her anger and his, all he could think about was how right it had felt to be with her. Until the vampire had emerged. Until she had revealed her own lies.

He knew all about what deceit did to a relationship, how any relationship built on lies couldn't survive. Just look at his own life. Only this time the pain was greater than that visited on him by his wife's betrayal. Physically healing was much easier than healing the heart.

He regretted that he had hurt Ramona, but he was just as enraged about what she had done to him.

Now he wanted to hurt and be hurt without impunity. He wanted to remind himself of the pain that came from choosing love poorly.

He knew just the place to satisfy that need.

The Blood Bank jumped with the pulse of the underworld as he walked in. Or maybe he was just more sensitized to the undead energy thanks to the raw pain surging through every pore of his body.

Ramona was dying. Her matter-of-fact confession still rang in his ears, and he still felt as if someone had driven a red-hot poker through his gut.

Diego needed to replace that grief with something he could forget come morning, when another day dawned for him and another slipped away for her.

Pushing through the crowd, he stalked to the tables near the back room where the vamps and more determined humans lingered. He was not disappointed as his gaze settled on the variety of lesser vampires and humans who lurked there, waiting to be chosen, hoping for someone to take them into one of the back rooms and satisfy their baser hungers.

He had barely contained his demon upon his arrival at the club, and the lingering thrum of that inhuman power clung to him, calling to vampire and human alike.

He skipped past the undead, needing satisfaction from a mortal tonight. The demon hungered for the taste of the blood it had been deprived of earlier.

Standing by one table, he noticed two women just ahead of him, dressed in their best impression of vamp attire with lots of black leather, laced tightly to show off their ample assets. Their arms were draped around each other. Even from there, he could smell their arousal.

When he neared, one woman she smiled, aware that she and her friend had his attention. He insinuated himself between the two of them, kissing one and groaning as the other reached around and unerringly found his erection.

"Come with me," he said, knowing that the owner of the club wouldn't appreciate him finishing this little ménage in full view of the club. Not that Foley wouldn't mind viewing the display himself, but even at the Blood Bank there were rules, minimal though they may be.

He grasped the women's hands and they followed him past the vampire guard, who knew better than to ask Diego for the customary fee. There would be time enough on another day to settle the bill.

With a kick at a semiopen door, Diego jerked the women ahead of him, and before he could undo their clothes, they were both on him, stripping him of his. He knew then that he had made his selection well.

Tonight wasn't about pleasure. He wasn't even sure it was about pain, but that would be a good start.

He walked them to the bed and tossed one woman onto it, where he shackled her to the posts and tore off her pants. From the corner of his eye, he noted her friend eagerly surveying the choice of toys on the wall and the leather and metal at her hip. She had brought her own toys to play with.

"Pick well, my love," he said to her, even as he slipped between her friend's legs. He thrust into her repeatedly until the first lash fell against his back.

He froze then, the pain tightening his gut, reminding him of why he was here. Because he was undead physically, and emotionally empty.

"More," he said, wanting the punishment to salve his conscience. With each lash against his back and every thrust into the willing body beneath him he was reminded that love and pain were irrevocably entwined. That to avoid the pain, he had to push away the love.

He released the vampire and sank his fangs deep into the prone woman's neck, feeding from her. The sex-charged blood raced through him, pulsing eagerly through his veins. As her body went limp, he dragged his mouth from her neck and pulled himself from her, still erect and still unsatisfied.

He turned to her friend, despite his feeding he was feeling light-headed, almost weak. He shook his head and finally allowed himself to fully appreciate the fire searing his back, the drip of blood from where she had stripped the skin from him with the whip she held in her hand.

A whip studded with small silver barbs.

He realized then why the weakness grew with each passing moment. The silver had delayed his vamp healing. Only feeding more might help.

But with every second that elapsed he weakened.

He moved toward the woman and she lashed out at him again, catching him across the chest with the whip. He cried out in pain, but she drew back her arm, readying herself for another blow.

With an explosion of speed, he snared her arm and carried her back against the wall. She laughed loudly, almost madly, and licked at the blood running from the slashes in his chest while dropping the whip. Before he realized her intent, she snared a silver dagger from a sheath on her belt and plunged it into his side. The knife vibrated against a rib bone before sliding deep.

Diego staggered back, clutching the hilt, and she picked up the whip again, advancing on him.

"Like to play, do you? Like to bite? We can bite back, you know," she said, anger coloring her words and bloodlust spurring her attack.

He barely had time to raise an arm to block the blow. The silver barbs raked furrows in his forearm, and he stumbled back, legs unsteady.

As he fell to the floor, his vision beginning to fade from the pain and loss of blood, he thought he saw something race past him. The sound of flesh striking flesh snagged his attention and he saw the woman fly across the room and into the wall. Her head connected with a loud thud and she dropped to ground, dazed, but still alive.

Hand on the hilt of the knife, which he was too weak to draw out, he looked upward as a shadow fell across him. Surprise filled him as he realized who had come to his aid.

"Stacia? Didn't know you were back," he said, trying to seem nonchalant before the vamp elder. But he coughed after he finished, bringing up blood. The dagger had pierced his lung, and when he sucked in a breath, he heard a gurgle welling in his chest.

"*Mio amico.* What were you thinking? I could hear your pain in my head from nearly across town." Stacia knelt beside him and gently eased his hand away from the knife buried deep in his side.

"Wanted to hurt," he somehow managed to say, each word taxing his failing energy. He almost wished that the connection he shared with Stacia—a connection created because they had fed on each other and often—hadn't alerted her to his troubles.

"You managed that quite well, my love." Stacia swiftly jerked the knife from his side, dragging a ragged gasp from him.

His vision blurred again. She cradled him in her arms, and he protested as fresh waves of pain erupted across his back.

"Feed. It will help you heal," she said, and suddenly her wrist was at his mouth, urging him to suckle. Only Diego knew that Stacia's help likely came with a stiff price.

Certainly stiff, my love. She mentally broadcast the message visions of what she wanted and flooded his mind, assaulting him while bringing intense physical need.

He opened his mouth and barely grazed her wrist with his fangs. But she once again exhorted him to strengthen himself so that he might later satisfy his need and hers, raping his mind with visions of the payment she would demand and he couldn't refuse.

Stacia was an elder, and with her power, whatever she wanted, she could have. That she was willing to feed him in return was more than she gave most.

Biting down, careful of the seemingly fragile bones of her arm beneath his mouth, he sucked. The first taste of her blood surged through his body, numbing the pain from his wounds. With each drag of his mouth, her blood energized every cell within him.

The demon sensed his body repairing itself, and as the discomfort and injuries fled, a knot of physical need grew deep in his loins.

Physical because he knew that the satisfaction that came, much like that from the woman he had taken earlier, would be empty. Devoid of any meaning without the emotion he had experienced with Ramona earlier.

Just as only blood could sustain his body, possibly only Ramona could feed his soul.

As Stacia sensed the change in him, she encircled his erection, her hand stroking surely before she let him ease back to the cold floor of the room. When her gaze met his, Diego knew it was time for payment.

In no time he had pleasured her to the brink of completion. But he knew only one thing would bring true release to each of them, because only blood truly called to their hearts.

Burying his head against the madly beating pulse at her neck, he sank his fangs deep, as she did, and the ardor of the vampire's kiss swept through him.

It was as it should be, he thought. Pleasure and pain. Blood and sex.

The vampire way. A puny human like Ramona had no place in such an existence.

Chapter 14

"This will definitely add to your tab," Foley said.

Silence reigned for a moment as they took in the condition of the room. Blood had splattered against two of the walls and stained a rather large section of the cement floor. The blood—beginning to turn rusty-colored as it dried—also smeared the skin of the two women shackled to the thick iron posts of the bed.

After a quick nip of Diego's attacker to insure her forgetfulness, Stacia and he had secured the one to avoid her waking and getting bloodthirsty again, while Stacia fed him yet a third time to strengthen him. Even now, his skin felt raw and the dull ache in his side reminded him that he was still not healed completely.

Foley rushed to the women and checked their pulses. Seemingly satisfied that they would be fine, he jabbed a finger in Diego's direction. "Look at this mess. Who's going to pay to clean it up?"

At that, Stacia made a tsking sound. She mimicked choking Foley, and suddenly he clutched at his throat, struggling for air.

"You should learn to respect your elders."

Diego placed his hand on her arm. "Please let him go. He knows he need not worry about whether I will take care of payment."

Stacia tossed Foley against the doorjamb with barely a flicker of her hand. "Go. Diego and I have some unfinished business."

"There's no need for you to linger, Stacia. I will have a glass or two from Foley's stash."

He sensed her pique at his dismissal. Had he been anyone else, he suspected Stacia would have drained him dry and watched with glee as his body shriveled to dust. But they had a long history, and in a way that not even the oldest of vampires could understand, were friends. Of course, as his elder, and a vampire with no desire to keep her humanity, Stacia might rather think of them as friends with feeding privileges.

Just as she had allowed him to feed from her tonight, if she required it, he would return the favor without hesitation.

I know, she broadcast into his head. With a sad smile, she waved and surged from the room in a blur of motion, leaving him to face Diana and Ryder, who were waiting at the bar.

The two of them took seats on either side of him, shutting him off from the inquiring eyes. Clearly, the action in the special rooms had garnered attention, maybe too much, which was likely why Foley had called Ryder and Diana to come down. While the Blood Bank liked to cater to a certain clientele, it also relied on the inherent disbelief in creatures such as vampires, hence why even here there was one rule—don't drain the humans. The bodies were just too hard to hide.

Thankfully, a vampire's bite brought forgetfulness, as well, eliminating the short-term memory of those who chose to make themselves willing snacks.

Hunching over to further avoid the limelight, Diego regretted the movement as agony erupted across the muscles in his back. Pain too similar to what he had experienced five hundred years earlier.

But you wanted the pain, the voice in his head reminded him. *You wanted the punishment for not being human. For not being able to love the mortal.*

"Diego." Diana covered his hand with hers gently. Slightly chilly, her touch sent an unusual tingle of vamp power through him. One that said Ryder had bitten her more than he should have.

"Tell us what happened. When Foley called us—"

"Foley needs to mind his own business." Diego waved for one of the vamp bartenders to bring over a glass.

"He heard the noises in the back. When Stacia went in—"

"She saved me. Not that it matters much. She sensed I needed help, and came when one of you mortal types got a little too eager."

Diana obviously didn't fail to hear the disdain in his voice for those of her kind. "Ms. Escobar has obviously pissed you off in a major way. Why don't you tell us how and whether we're still supposed to help?"

The waiter placed the wineglass filled with blood before Diego and he chugged it down.

"The lady is dying. That's what humans do. That's what women do. They die. Like Esperanza did. Like Ramona and Diana will," he snarled, lashing out in anger and pain.

He never saw the fist that knocked him out cold.

She hadn't slept well.

The smell of him had clung to her skin and her sheets. A shower and change of bedding hadn't helped.

Every time she closed her eyes, images of his vampire face invaded.

Diego was a vampire. A living—although some wouldn't consider it living, his being undead and all—breathing, bloodsucking vampire. She didn't want to think that the last place his fangs had been were right at her neck.

Only he hadn't bitten her.

No, he'd made love to her amazingly. She still felt a slight tenderness between her legs as she sat in the hard plastic chair outside Melissa Danvers's office.

Dr. Melissa Danvers. Sister-in-law to FBI Agent Diana Reyes. Diana who was Diego's friend. Was Melissa Diego's friend, also? It made Ramona wonder whether Diana and Ryder were vampires, too. They all had a similar pale look about them.

Or maybe it was her imagination working overtime again, the same way it had at every creak she had heard the night before as she'd lain in bed, trying to sleep.

Melissa's nurse and assistant, Sara, came down the hall, her sneakered feet squeaking on the shiny tiles of the hospital corridor. She lifted the file in her hand and said, "I've got the new lab results here. Why don't you come with me?"

Sara opened the door to Melissa's office, ushered Ramona in and then left, closing the door behind her.

"How are you this morning? You look tired," Melissa said as she opened the file Sara had deposited on her desk, and began to flip through the papers.

"I am tired. I didn't sleep much."

Melissa frowned as she peered at the test results. "I'm assuming the lack of sleep has something to do with needing my sister-in-law's help."

"Dead cell phone battery was too lame an excuse, huh?" Ramona quipped, trying to appear unruffled. She quickly perused Melissa's desktop, noting the framed photos, one of which included Diana and Ryder. Another had a shot of Melissa, a baby and a man who bore a striking resemblance to Diana, although he had a tanned and smiling face.

"I met them last night. A mutual friend, Diego Rivera, thought Diana could help me with a problem I was having," she explained, waiting for Melissa to jump in and offer more information. But she didn't. Instead, Melissa buried her head in the file, so Ramona pressed on.

"Diego revealed his true self to me last night. Kinda scary."

The papers rattled in Melissa's hand and she slowly lowered them. "You know he's a vampire?"

"That's what he told me he was. Of course, it was easy to believe, what with the glowing eyes and immense white fangs."

With a deep sigh, the doctor leaned back in her chair. "I was pretty freaked myself the first time I saw it."

"Diana and Ryder. They're just like Diego, right?"

Melissa chuckled harshly. "Some criminals might think my sister-in-law is one scary bitch, but she's totally human."

"But Ryder is a vampire?" Ramona waved her hand, urging the young doctor to explain.

With another deep sigh, Melissa leaned forward in her chair and laced her fingers together over the file. "I am…or at least I *was*…Ryder's keeper."

Ramona had never heard the term before, so Melissa explained. "A keeper is a human who takes care of a vampire's needs, like getting blood. He or she also protects the vampire when he's not awake, and takes care of other mundane tasks."

"But you're not his keeper anymore?"

"When my daughter, Mariel, was born, Ryder released me from that obligation. But how do you stop caring for someone who's like family? Who you've known your whole life?"

Melissa's anguish touched Ramona, reminding her that the reality of Diego's existence had consequences that reached beyond her. It impacted on other lives, and sometimes not in a good way.

"You don't stop caring," she said, a slightly dazed tone in her voice that the doctor immediately seized upon.

"You still have feelings for Diego."

Did she? For so many years Ramona had been attracted to him. It had been purely physical at first, but then she had discovered his honor and his caring spirit. She had come to enjoy his wit and ability to appreciate the art he so passionately championed at his gallery.

Last night, at the height of their desire, she had even thought for a moment that she might love him. That she could imagine spending the rest of her life with him. Her probably short life, she thought, and gestured to the file on Melissa's desk—the main reason she was sitting there today. Not that she hadn't appreciated the enlightening discussion about Melissa's family and friends.

"What do the tests say?"

Melissa rubbed one hand across the top of the file and met her gaze head-on. "That we need to be more aggressive. Are you prepared to do that?"

Ramona thought of the danger to her mother, which needed to be resolved. Of the painting of Diego, sitting only partially completed in her loft. Last, but definitely not least, she thought of Diego and the harsh way last night had ended. She knew she had to make some things right between them before…

"*Sí,* I'm prepared to do that. Just tell me what I need to do."

Chapter 15

When she called the gallery, the receptionist mentioned that Diego wouldn't be in until late that afternoon.

Ramona hadn't thought his hours odd before. Nor had she taken his leaving so early the other morning as anything other than the actions of a busy man. Now his pattern took on new meaning.

Horror movie lore said that vampires and sunlight didn't mix. Obviously not accurate, since Diego seemed able to be out during certain daylight hours.

As she sat on her stool in front of her easel, the early afternoon light spilled in through the sky-lights, flooding the loft with warm golden rays. She picked up some oil paint with her brush and laid it on the canvas, recreating the light and shadows of Diego's body. As she did so, she realized his flesh would never experience that luminous glow.

Where was he now? Tucked into a coffin somewhere by his keeper?

A knock came at her door.

She carefully put down her brush and palette and walked to the door, where she peered through the peephole.

Diana Reyes sans vampire escort.

Ramona rolled open the door and the agent took that as an invitation to enter. She glanced around, then walked over to the painting of Diego in the altogether. "Impressive," she said.

Hard to deny, Ramona thought as she joined her before the easel. "Yes, he is quite handsome."

Diana stifled a chuckle. "I was talking about your painting. Not the subject matter."

Heat swept up her neck and across her cheeks, but she restrained herself from covering her face with her paint-smudged hands. Drawing a calming breath, she eased onto her stool and picked up her brushes and palette, intending to use her painting as a shield. "As you can see, I'm busy."

"Too busy to hear what I've got on van Winter so far?"

Ramona paused with the brush halfway to the canvas. "I wasn't sure you were really going to help me."

"Got some coffee? I didn't get my Starbucks fix this morning."

Neither had she. After taking the new drugs Melissa had prescribed, she'd found her stomach too unsettled for much of anything, especially coffee. A nice *café con leche* might be just the thing right now, however.

"Sure," she said, once again putting away her supplies.

Diana followed her to the kitchen, taking a stool by the island as Ramona made the coffee.

Looking over her shoulder as she got out some mugs, she asked, "Sugar?"

"As much as is humanly possible."

Diana's comment dragged a smile to Ramona's lips. "A woman after my own heart."

"In more ways than you can imagine," she stated.

Ramona finished making the hot drinks, brought them over and placed one before Diana. "How do you figure?"

"You're in love with Diego. I know how hard it can be to love a vampire."

"He told you about last night?"

Diana nodded, and when she reached for the coffee, Ramona noticed the large bruise across the other woman's knuckles. "Occupational hazard?"

The FBI agent's smile widened into a satisfied grin. "Nah. I just needed to remind someone about his manners."

Ramona didn't ask for details, opting to turn the discussion to the business between them. After taking a bracing sip of her coffee, she said, "I'm surprised that you're still willing to help, considering that you know what happened between Diego and me."

With a shrug, Diana said, "Friends don't desert friends."

"Diego isn't my friend anymore."

"But Melissa is." The agent took a sip and winced at the heat of the coffee.

"I don't want Melissa involved in what's going on with van Winter."

"I don't, either. Van Winter is dangerous," Diana said.

"And you've come to this realization how?"

Diana put the mug down. "Instinct. Plus some things just don't make sense."

"Like what?" Ramona asked, wrapping her hands around the mug because of the sudden nip at her core.

"I ferreted out some financials on the appraiser and transport company. Nothing out of the ordinary in any of the information I could access."

"So they're not involved?" Ramona asked, wondering where the switch had been made. "What if the art transport company didn't pack the originals?"

"They didn't." Diana explained how, according to the movers, van Winter had had his own staff pack the paintings. The movers had only picked up the three crates for delivery to the auction house.

"So van Winter loaded the copies in the crates, but we have no way of proving it."

A grin lit up Diana's features. "Not yet. If you can think of anything, call me," she said, and rose from the stool. She reached into the pocket of her black suit jacket and placed a business card on the island.

"How can I thank you?" Ramona said.

"Don't give up. Not on life. Not on Diego."

Diego roused himself, the waning of the afternoon sun calling him to rise and prepare for another night. One that would hopefully be better than the night before.

Simon had been asleep when he returned from the Blood Bank shortly after three in the morning, hours earlier than normal from a night out. Diego had opted not to wake the old man, totally capable of removing from the fridge a bag of blood from the butcher.

He had sucked it down quickly, the taste of the cold beef's blood not as appealing as a warm human's.

As he turned over in bed, only a faint protest came from his muscles, confirming that the bulk of the damage done the night before had healed. The various feedings and Stacia's intervention had helped his body repair from the blows of the whip, plus the knifing. Running his hand over his side, he felt the phantom pain of that injury and chastised himself for his carelessness. He had allowed his emotions to distract him, and that distraction had nearly proved fatal.

He couldn't allow it to happen again.

The only way to make certain of that was to not see Ramona again. His emotions around her were too raw, too conflicted.

As he swung his legs over the side of the bed, Simon hobbled in, leaning heavily on the ornate mahogany butler's cart bearing Diego's breakfast—a large glass of blood.

"How are you today?" Diego asked, noting that his steps seemed slower, more laborious.

"I'm tired, sir. I don't think it will be too long now," his keeper said, rousing unwelcome emotion within Diego.

He still had trouble understanding how Simon could be so accepting of his fate, and yet he understood that in some ways death provided a peace and closure that his eternal life never would.

Death brought a human's life full circle, from cradle to grave. Diego watched that cycle from his undead existence and understood that it was the way it should be. His nearly immortal state perverted the natural order of things.

While he had prayed to escape the death visited on him by the Inquisitor, he now understood the price he had paid, the toll it had taken on Esperanza and others like them.

"Master?" Simon asked, and Diego realized that

his keeper had been waiting for him to have his feeding and go on with his day.

"I'm sorry, Simon. I was just thinking."

"About something sad, sir. I could see it in your eyes." The old man knew him well after nearly a century together.

"It will pass," Diego said as he picked up the goblet and took a sip. Human blood and perfectly warmed. He morphed and sucked it down greedily. When he was done, he slipped back to his human state and dabbed at his lips with the linen napkin beside the glass. It came away with smudges of his meal.

Disgust filled him at the sight. At the reminder of what he was and would forever be. Loneliness came next as he met Simon's slightly rheumy gaze and noticed the tremble in his thin hands on the handle of the cart.

"Go rest, my friend. I have some errands to run," Diego said, and the old man left the bedroom, his gait almost painful to behold.

Diego rose from the bed and quickly dressed. He had to get to the gallery and make sure all was in order, but he knew he wouldn't linger.

Ramona's paintings would be there, slated to hang for another couple of days before being shipped to their respective buyers. They'd had a sellout show, but that brought no happiness. He knew now why Ramona had needed the exhibit so quickly, why she'd needed the money. She wanted to put her house in order before she died.

Because that's what humans did, he thought again and winced. He rubbed his chin as the memory of Diana's blow came back to him. The lady packed quite a wallop. He still couldn't fathom Ryder's allegiance to her, couldn't comprehend that his friend willingly subjected himself to a relationship with only one possible outcome.

No, not just one.

His friend could turn Diana, much like Diego had sired Esperanza. Much like he could bestow the kiss of eternal life on Ramona.

He forced that thought from his mind as he left his apartment and headed down to the street to flag a cab. Eternal life brought with it many difficulties. Only the strongest individuals could deal with it, and even then, the constant loss and change burdened your soul, made you shut off a piece of yourself at a time, until all humanity was gone.

It was why the elders were so dangerous. No trace of humanity remained within them. Vampires like Stacia no longer felt anything human, no longer understood the joys of life. Only blood called to them or brought satisfaction.

As Diego thought about the centuries to come in his life—centuries alone—he wondered whether he, too, would lose his humanity. Or whether he'd become like some others he had known and walk out into the sun, never to return to the darkness of eternal life.

He paused outside his apartment building and

looked up at the late afternoon sun, already low in the horizon. He was old enough to tolerate such weak sunshine, but still, pins and needles pricked the exposed parts of his skin. He stretched his hands outward and closed his eyes, a supplicant to the sun and its power, until its touch became painful.

Then he snapped into action, striding briskly to the curb and hailing a cab. Once inside, he scooted to the center of the seat, away from the light.

Ramona's sunny apartment came to mind. It would be warm and golden with both morning and afternoon light, thanks to the skylights. He imagined those rays bathing her as he lay with her in bed, touching her skin and warming it, bringing a flush of color with their kiss.

She would never again experience those things if she became like him.

He wouldn't do it. Couldn't do it. He cared for her too much to bring her into a world that would deny her children and the joy of growing old.

But fate already denied her those things. He thrust that reality far away because it complicated everything.

No matter how hard you tried, fate had a way of catching up with you. The longer you avoided it, the more it screwed you up when it finally found you.

Just look at me, he thought. Possibly in love with a human. A dying human.

What better punishment could fate deliver?

Chapter 16

Ramona paused outside the steps to the gallery. The lights from the display windows illuminated the sidewalk, calling to her. She looked upward, her arms wrapped tightly around herself to battle the chill. One of her smaller pieces hung in the window, along with information about the current showing. Beyond the painting, she could see a few people in the front room, walking from piece to piece.

The show had been a success. Diego's assistant had called to say all of the paintings had been sold, and for quite a nice sum. Ramona had made arrangements for the check to be sent to the trust fund she had set up. That money would be enough to take care of her mother for some time.

Now she had to take care of her own life, or what was left of it. She had to straighten out the mess she had made of things, including the man—no, make that vampire—who waited inside the gallery.

She checked her watch. Only a half hour remained until the gallery closed its doors. Just enough time for her to go in and apologize for her lies.

Her steps hesitant, she walked straight to the receptionist's desk. The young woman there, elegantly dressed in a cowl-necked black knit dress, smiled broadly. "Ms. Escobar. It's a joy to see you."

A few heads turned their way and people leaned closer, their whispered comments tinged with excitement. She had never quite gotten used to such attention. Forcing a smile, she acknowledged their stares with what she hoped was a cordial nod.

Returning her gaze to Diego's receptionist, she said, "I was hoping Mr. Rivera had a moment."

"For you, of course."

The young woman rose from her chair, but Ramona gestured for her to sit. "I know the way."

She almost felt as if she was walking to the gallows as she passed through each room, pausing for one last glimpse of the largest painting. The one she had come to think of as theirs.

Of course, nothing in her imagination as she'd painted it could have prepared her for the much better reality of Diego as a lover.

But then the unbidden image came. Diego as a vampire.

Ramona's hand trembled as she knocked once, briskly, on his office door.

A muffled "Come in" greeted her, but she delayed, suddenly uncertain if this was wise.

A moment later the door flew open and he stood there, the practiced smile on his face turning to a scowl as he realized who it was.

"What do you want?" he asked, his voice a low rumble. As she met his gaze, the ice-blue of his eyes slowly bled out to the scary blue-green neon of the demon, and a menacing hint of fang dropped from his top lip.

"You can't scare me away, Diego."

She hoped she sounded calm, in control, strong. Someone like him wouldn't abide weakness. Her gut tightened with trepidation as if to taunt her, but she fought back her fear. Something told her he would never hurt her.

Diego examined her. He let his vamp senses take in everything about her. The weaker beat of her heart and the chill in her body that went beyond the cooler temperature of the night air outside. A bright slash of color stained each cheek, but beyond that blush her skin was pale.

"I thought you never wanted to see me again."

"Diana came by this afternoon. She told me she was working on the case. I wanted to say thank-you." Ramona plucked at the sleeves of her coat, clearly uneasy.

"Diana has a mind of her own. She would do

what she wanted regardless of what I said." He kept his tone cold, almost cruel, because anything else would move them toward perilous ground.

She winced as if struck, and the color fled from her face. Despite that, she gathered herself, pulling her shoulders back beneath the loose folds of her dark-blue peacoat. She walked toward him and cradled his jaw.

He flinched, her touch cold on his skin.

She rose on tiptoe and whispered against his lips, "I'm sorry I lied, but I'm not sorry about us. About what happened."

In the space of a heartbeat, she kissed him and then fled.

Diego remained rooted to the floor, his hands balled into fists, his gut twisted into a knot. He took a faltering step, about to follow her, and then remembered the lunacy of caring for a human.

Holding fast, his muscles trembling from the strain, he reached out with his vamp senses and picked up the lingering remnants of her scent and the hurried *lub-dub* of her heart as she raced away.

Closing his eyes, he focused on it, memorized its beat until it faded from hearing.

As it would fade when she died.

Ramona mumbled a rushed goodbye to the receptionist as she hurried out the door. She had gone half a block before she slowed her pace, wondering why she was bothering to rush.

She had no one waiting for her at home. Nothing to do except work on Diego's painting and hope that her stomach would settle down, because the second dose Melissa had prescribed was wreaking havoc on her system.

Pausing for a deep breath, she heard the muffled ring of her cell phone from her coat pocket, and yanked it out.

"Hello."

"Rather chilly night for a walk, isn't it, Ms. Escobar?" Van Winter's tone was obsequious, but his words worried her. Pivoting on her heel, she peered up and down the street, but it seemed to be business as usual on the Soho block. A few passing cars and pedestrians. Over on Broadway, the higher volume of traffic, both automotive and on foot, moved swiftly by.

"What do you want, Mr. van Winter?" she said, but kept her eyes on the road, vigilant after being nearly run over a week earlier. She had no doubt van Winter had been behind that near accident.

"Come now, Ramona. You can call me Frederick by now, don't you think?"

"What do you want, Frederick?" she asked, and began walking rapidly toward Broadway, thinking she would be safer there with the increased activity.

Van Winter finally said, "You've been seeing a lot of Mr. Rivera lately. Too much."

"Mr. Rivera sells my works. That's it." She wanted to shift attention from Diego, afraid of what van Winter might do. Afraid of how vulnerable Diego's vampire state made him.

"He's been asking questions and it has to stop, Ramona. Do you understand?" In the background she heard an approaching siren. Much like the one now moving closer as she finally turned the corner onto Broadway.

She ended the connection and backed toward the window of one shop, guarding her back as she looked for the late-model black sedan that had nearly run her over the other night.

She saw nothing until the light changed and the cars slowly stopped. Then a familiar stretch limo came into view. It had picked her up many a time to take her to van Winter's building so she could work.

Her phone rang again. She answered. "What do you want?"

"Ramona?" This was a woman's voice, and she immediately identified herself. "It's Diana Reyes."

"This isn't a good time," Ramona said as the light turned green. The limo inched forward slowly and drew up to the bus stop before her.

"Are you okay?" the agent asked.

"Van Winter is here." The mirrored window of the backseat sluggishly lowered, and there he was, smiling his cold, snakelike grin.

"Where's 'here'?" Diana demanded. "Can you keep him there?"

"He's in a limo and I'm on foot. Doubt it."

Van Winter quirked his index finger, beckoning her closer. Before Ramona went, she murmured, "I'm putting it on speakerphone. Stay quiet."

She tucked the phone into the pocket of her purse and slung the bag over her shoulder, praying the position would allow Diana to hear their conversation, and hoping van Winter would say something that the agent could use to build a case. Faking a confident stride, Ramona approached the limo.

"Mr. van Winter. How can I help you tonight?"

"Call off Rivera and whatever other dogs you have sniffing around."

"And what if I don't?"

Van Winter gave a phlegmy laugh, then coughed before he said, "You have nothing to gain and everything to lose."

His comment drew a jerky chuckle from her. "Everything to lose? I'm as good as dead. How much worse could it be, Frederick?" she asked, accenting each syllable of his name.

"You got the package I sent, didn't you? Think about that."

Then he waved at his driver and put up the mirrored glass as the limo muscled its way into the traffic.

"Did you hear that?" she said out loud, and then slipped her fingers into her purse to remove her cell phone.

"Most of it. What's the package he's referring to?"

"The envelope and photos we gave you last night," she confirmed.

"We got several fingerprints off the photos. I'll need to print you and Diego so we can eliminate yours."

Ramona walked back to the corner and peered down the street toward the gallery, wondering if she should go warn Diego. Then she rethought it. Now that the adrenaline of the meeting had faded away, her stomach had started a weird kind of rumbling. "I'm not really up to it tonight. Can I meet you somewhere tomorrow?"

"I have a few calls to make in the morning. How about a late lunch? Luigi's near Federal Plaza."

"Deal."

Ryder rolled Diego's thumb in the ink and then moved it to the card, where he rotated it against the paper to record its print. He repeated the procedure until all of his friend's fingerprints were on the sheet. Smiling, Ryder said, "All done," and handed him a premoistened wipe to clean his hands.

Diego mangled the small cloth as he rubbed at his fingers, trying to remove all the ink. "I'm glad. Why didn't your little friend come and do this herself?"

Unexpectedly, Ryder's smile broadened. "Because I didn't want to see you get hurt again."

He snorted in disbelief, but then realized Ryder wasn't kidding. "Is that what intrigues you? Her violence?"

His friend shook his head. "She definitely intrigues me, *amigo.* As for violence, her edge can be quite sharp at times."

"Is that why you're so determined to endure the pain of a mortal's love?" Diego said as he rose and walked to the small bar at the edge of Ryder's office. Perusing the offerings, he realized his friend kept no blood there.

Pouring brandy into two snifters, he waited for an answer, but it didn't come. He returned to the desk and handed him a glass. "So, why do you do this?"

Ryder raised his snifter and said, "When love calls, only a fool refuses to answer."

"Love," he said with a sniff. After taking a sip of the brandy, he retorted, "You confuse the call of her blood with what you think is love."

Ryder shook his head. "Foolish Diego. How long will you deny it?"

"Can you deny that you've bitten her?"

"No, I can't. Can you be as truthful?" Ryder challenged.

"Blood, *amigo.* It's what sustains us. Nothing else will satisfy."

To which his friend replied, "Liar."

Chapter 17

Ramona hugged the toilet bowl as her body spasmed over and over. By the time she finished, she was drenched in cold sweat and her limbs trembled with weakness. She struggled to her knees, then somehow found the strength to get to her feet. Her steps slow, she shuffled to the sink, where she rinsed her face and mouth.

She stripped off the sweat-dampened clothes and turned on the shower. When the water was deliciously hot, she stepped in and just stood there, letting it warm her. The chill she'd felt was due to so much more than the medicines battling with her out-of-control immune system.

Van Winter's threat had troubled her all night long, robbing her of badly needed sleep.

She wondered whether Diana would have any information later that afternoon, and thought about what the agent had said the day before—that the transport company hadn't packed the artwork.

There hadn't been that many people van Winter had allowed near her when she'd been doing the copies. Who among them had he trusted to pack the works? Even more importantly, who had he gotten to sign them?

Finishing up, she stepped from the shower and started her day.

First thing on her list was calling Melissa to tell her about her body's reactions to the cocktail of medicines.

The doctor answered on the second ring. "How are you?"

"A little sick," Ramona said, and tucked the phone between her ear and shoulder as she put the kettle on the stove, hoping some chamomile tea would help soothe her stomach.

"A little or a lot?"

Reluctantly, she admitted, "A lot. I can't keep the morning mix down at all. The afternoon dose lingers a little longer. But only a little."

Melissa hesitated, but then quickly rattled off an adjustment, splitting the doses into three. "Make sure not to skip a dose. They're keeping everything in balance until—"

"I'm not hoping for that donor to miraculously appear, Melissa. I have to have my head straight about this, not filled with unrealistic possibilities."

"Then what made you change your mind about looking for one? Why even embrace that hope?" the doctor asked.

"I thought I had something more… I was wrong."

With that, she hung up. The teakettle whistled, the sound becoming a hissing screech as she stood there, considering what she had told Melissa.

She had thought she'd found love. Love made everything possible.

Even beating death.

Located a few blocks from Federal Plaza, Luigi's was an old-fashioned Italian restaurant, much like one might find on the rapidly vanishing streets of Little Italy, which were being swallowed by an ever-expanding Chinatown.

A quick look revealed that Diana had yet to arrive, so Ramona loitered inside the front door, checking out the menu posted there. Her stomach grumbled—in a good way, thanks to her medicine change—at the thought of a nice plate of chicken parmigiana.

The front door opened, allowing a bright beam of light into the darkened interior, and Diana entered, dressed as usual in a dark suit and white shirt. When the agent noticed Ramona standing there, she smiled and walked over. "Glad you could make it."

"Diana, *mia amica.* So good to see you," the hostess said. The Rubenesque older woman stepped around the podium and embraced her in meaty arms.

"Nice to see you, too. Do you have a table for us?" Diana asked.

"Your usual." She ushered them to a booth toward the back of the restaurant.

"Come here often?" Ramona teased after they were seated.

"Not as much as I used to, unfortunately," Diana replied.

"Busy at work?"

"Actually, no. I'm on modified assignment right now."

The hesitancy and distress in the agent's voice was apparent despite the barrier of the menu. Ramona put hers down and examined Diana's face. She was about to question her further when a handsome young waiter arrived and placed a large basket of garlic bread in the middle of the table. There was no denying the garlicy aroma that wafted toward them.

Diana pointed at the bread. "That's part of the reason why I don't come here as often."

Garlic and vampires. Apparently horror movie lore wasn't that far off the money. "So what's the other part?"

"At first work, but now mainly my involvement with Ryder," Diana said, and snagged a piece of garlic bread from the basket.

Ramona didn't want to get into the whole relationship-with-a-vampire topic. "So you're on modified assignment. What does that mean?"

Diana chewed a bite of bread slowly, almost thoughtfully, before she finally said, "It basically means I screwed up and I'm on desk duty. Security clearance checks and that kind of thing."

The waiter came over and, with a wink at Diana, said, "The usual, *bella?*"

"The usual."

Ramona placed her order for the chicken parmigiana and immediately resumed the conversation. "How are you working—"

"On your case? Unofficially. At some point I may have to turn this over to the FBI Art Crime Team, but not until you and your *mami* are safe," Diana said.

Ramona hesitated, unsure of what to say. Van Winter was a powerful man with many high-level connections. "How can you be certain?"

Diana leaned her forearms on the table and shifted closer. "I can't be sure, but I also can't arrange for protective custody until I have more information."

"What do you need besides the fingerprints?"

The waiter came over with their plates. There was silence for a few minutes as they sampled their meals, and then Diana commenced her explanation. "I did some searches to see if anything unusual was going on with our friend. He filed a police report about a week after the paintings were moved to the auction house."

"What for?" Ramona asked, and twirled her fork in her pasta.

She had the fork halfway to her mouth when Diana said, "He claimed that a Luis Rodriguez stole several small objet d'art from his penthouse."

"I met Luis when I was working on the paintings. He was a hardworking family man."

Diana nodded and ate a piece of a large prawn from her plate of garlic-infused scampi. "No priors, but his bank account had an unusual deposit a few days after the police report was filed. A very large deposit."

"I don't believe it. Can't you question him?" She recalled the gentle man who had been a servant in van Winter's apartment. Luis had always made sure she was comfortable and would sometimes share a coffee break with her, telling her about his family. In some ways, he had reminded her of her own father, with his softly accented English and work-rough hands.

Diana laid her fork down, picked up her water and took a large sip. When she put the glass down she said, "I can't. He's dead. Killed by a hit-and-run driver on his way home from a dishwashing job. Apparently van Winter fired him the same day he filed the police report."

Ramona's stomach immediately twisted with anguish. The food on her plate was half-eaten and would stay that way. Her appetite had fled.

"It was a black sedan, wasn't it?"

Diana curtly nodded. "Only witness was another dishwasher from the restaurant. They finished late, stepped outside and headed home in different directions."

"A black sedan came speeding out of nowhere and ran him down. If it hadn't been for Diego the other night, that might have happened to me," Ramona murmured numbly.

"I'll walk you home after this," Diana told her. "And once the sun isn't as strong, Ryder will swing by."

"That's not necessary. Actually, I might get kind of creeped out knowing Ryder was hanging from my rafters or something," she said, dragging a reluctant smile from the other woman.

"Ryder doesn't hang like a bat. I'm not sure if any of the vamps I'm acquainted with do, including Diego. He's hurting, you know."

"He's made himself quite clear and—"

Diana slashed a hand through the air. "Forget the vamp thing. It's a *man* thing. They will never admit to weakness."

Diego and *weak?* Not two words she would string together in the same sentence. Regardless of whether or not he actually had a weakness for her, Ramona could not allow herself any vulnerability around him.

"I've got other things to deal with now."

"Like my getting your prints. Best we do that back at your apartment. If van Winter is watching, this should look like two friends having lunch."

Ramona glanced around, but didn't notice anyone familiar. Then again, she hadn't noticed any of van Winter's goons in the last week, even though he clearly had his eyes and ears tuned to her goings-on.

"Agreed," she said, wondering just how much of what was left of her life van Winter was going to steal with his deception.

Chapter 18

The two deliverymen carefully transferred the crate with Ramona's painting onto a hand truck and grabbed their toolboxes. Diego followed them as they walked up to the door of Alicia Tipton's Upper West Side apartment building, where the doorman greeted them with familiarity and opened the door. Inside, a security guard likewise recognized the two men and efficiently checked off their names from a list.

Diego walked up next and handed the man his business card. The security guard scrutinized it, but said, "Picture ID?"

"He's with us, Louie. Wants to make sure we hang this painting just so for Mrs. Tipton," one deliveryman said.

At that the guard waved them on, and they walked to the freight elevator.

"I guess they know you here," Diego said as he scrutinized the men. Both were from the same transport company that had picked up the paintings from van Winter's Midtown penthouse.

"Mrs. Tipton has to approve everyone who comes and goes. We're the regulars for anything coming here."

"So you handled the auction house delivery for the van Winter sale?" he inquired, trying not to appear too nosy. The freight elevator slowly clanged its way to the penthouse. Through the gated door, he could count each level as it passed before them.

"Not everyone is bonded for the really expensive stuff, so we get to do all that work," one said, and from the corner of his eye, Diego noted how the thin man puffed his chest out with pride.

"Makes for nice tips, too," his brawnier friend interjected.

"Heard van Winter is a cheap old bastard," Diego said, and half turned so he could fully gauge their reactions.

"Stiffed us on our last pickup. Said we hadn't done any work, since his staff had packed up the paintings," Mr. Brawny replied with some annoyance.

The thin man screwed up his face, reminding Diego of a ferret. With an annoyed huff he said, "As if Luis could do as good a job as us."

Luis Rodriguez. The dead thief, Diego thought, recalling Diana's report from the night before. His death and supposed theft had made him the most likely candidate to be involved in switching the paintings. Now Diego had confirmed that. But it still didn't prove that Luis had done the switch, only that he had crated the paintings. Possibly the copies.

Diego played dumb. "Luis is…"

"Handyman. Manservant. You name it. He's at van Winter's beck and call," Ferret Face replied.

Diego judged from the man's use of the present tense that he was unaware of Luis's death. "Not anymore. I heard that one of van Winter's people was killed in a hit-and-run. I think that was the guy."

"Poor bastard. He'd just survived prostate cancer," Mr. Brawny said, shaking his head and mumbling again more softly, "Poor Luis."

"Yeah, and his youngest just starting college," his partner added.

A pattern seemed to be emerging, Diego thought. First Ramona, now Luis. Ill people in desperate straits. It only added to the possibility that Luis had switched the paintings, and made it more likely that van Winter had ordered the "accident."

As the elevator shuddered to a stop, Diego recalled the near hit-and-run Ramona had experienced. Van Winter clearly had no qualms about tying up loose ends.

The police report against Luis further insulated van Winter from any connection to the switch. What had he planned to do to implicate Ramona? Diego wondered as the brawny deliveryman shoved open the gate while his colleague threw the switch to open the exterior door.

The elevator opened onto a back hallway, and once they'd hauled out the hand truck and crate, the two men, well familiar with the layout of the floor, moved their burden to a door at one end and pushed a button. From the intercom came a tinny voice asking for identification. After they gave their names and Diego's, the door unlocked with a loud buzz.

Inside, the Tipton butler met them and led them to Alicia's private art gallery. At a pad by the door, he punched in a series of numbers to allow them entry. Within the room, walls and shelves were lined with an eclectic mix of art, including one of Ramona's earlier works that Diego had sold the heiress. The large room had been split in half by a partition whose pristine surface suggested it was new or had just been cleaned. Judging by the size of the wall, this was where Ramona's large canvas was to be hung.

As the men wheeled the hand truck toward that space, Alicia herself floated in wearing an exquisite charcoal-grey chiffon lounging garment that billowed about, adorning her fit, sixty-year-old body. She smiled and waved at the two deliverymen and then approached Diego, hugging him as she said, "I'm so glad you were able to personally oversee this."

The embrace lasted a little longer than was comfortable, until Diego managed to gently put some space between them. "My pleasure, Alicia. After all, as a lover of all things beautiful, how could I not come see you and your wonderful gallery?"

"Feel free to look around. Maybe you can stay for a late lunch?" Alicia asked, a hopeful tone in her voice.

Summoning all the skills that had made him one of Spain's more welcomed courtiers, he picked up her perfectly groomed hand, bent over it and dropped a kiss on the back. "It would be my pleasure."

With a girlish titter and a blush across her surgically enhanced cheekbones, she exited the room in another flourish of fabric. The scent of her expensive perfume lingered, as if to nag him about his deception.

As he faced the two deliverymen, their amused and sly glances annoyed him. He tamped down that emotion, having more important things to do. He might have distanced himself from Ramona, but his five-hundred-year-old promise to be a better man nagged at him to finish what he had begun, namely, proving her innocence.

With a wave of his hand, he instructed the two men to uncrate the work. While they did so, he sought out the masterpiece that Alicia had purchased from van Winter. Though Diego searched the exterior walls of the room, it was nowhere to be seen, so he walked around the partition and there it was, on the opposite side all by itself. Ironic, he thought. Two works by Ramona back-to-back.

Snagging his cell phone from his belt, he quickly snapped off a few pictures, which might help someone undertake a detailed analysis of the brushstrokes and proportions of the various figures in the work. Quite complicated methods had been devised for rating aspects of paintings, based on the discovery that artists tended to be predictable with certain details, such as the ratios of facial elements.

Bending, he sought out the signature in the bottom right-hand corner—a signature Ramona claimed she hadn't done. Getting as close as his camera phone would allow, he shot a photo or two before turning on the small light and snapping another few. No sense passing up the opportunity, since he might not get this chance again for a long time, if ever.

With that done, he e-mailed the photos to Diana, hoping she could tap her resources to begin the analysis of the masterpiece. He hoped it would confirm their suspicions that it was a copy, and that the signatures might provide some way to clear Ramona's name.

When his phone beeped, confirming receipt of the e-mails by Diana, he stepped around the partition and once again turned his attention to the deliverymen. They had unpacked the canvas and cleared away the crate to give themselves ample room to work.

Alicia had selected his favorite piece—the one that had led to his first kiss with Ramona. The one that when he closed his eyes for a vampire's version of slumber, played in his brain, reminding him of her passion. Of their passion, captured on the canvas for all the world to see.

There was only one thing better—the real deal.

He forced that thought away, considering how to hang the piece on the wall. He wasn't sure whether Alicia would want to put another work beside it, much as she had done on all the other walls save one—the one with what might possibly be a multimillion-dollar fake, if Ramona was right.

But then again, why else would van Winter be threatening her if she *wasn't* right?

Alicia returned at that moment and seemed to note his dilemma.

"It should hang alone, don't you think? All that ardor and hopefulness is singular."

Her words caught him off guard. He had seen the fervor of the lovers in the painting, but hopefulness? Glancing at the image once again, he was assailed by a flurry of memories. Of the first time he had met a much shyer Ramona, in her last year of art school. Of how she'd grown into the mature, poised woman who could create such wondrously moving art.

Unbidden came the vision of her beneath him, her eyes betraying her emotions as he made love to her. He saw, too, her last look of the other night, filled with love and so much more. Maybe there *was* hopefulness in the painting, hope as Alicia had so perceptively noted.

"It should hang alone," he confirmed.

The word from Melissa that morning was good. The new medicines had stabilized Ramona's cell counts, although keeping to the altered drug regimen was key to maintaining that stability. With the extra time, they might find a bone marrow donor and risk a transplant.

She was supposed to meet Diana again for lunch, at a place close to the hospital this time—a Mexican restaurant on Second Avenue. The agent apparently had some news. Good news, Ramona hoped, as the elevator deposited her in the hospital lobby and she exited onto York.

Getting her bearings, she realized she had to head downtown a few blocks before cutting west to Second. A few steps into the crosswalk, she saw a white delivery van come squealing around the corner right at her. Ramona immediately stepped back toward the safety of the curb, but bumped into someone right behind her. Someone big and muscular who covered her mouth with his hand and slipped a tree trunk of an arm around her waist.

The panel door of the van slid open violently as

the truck screeched to a halt before them. The man tossed her inside and then followed her. She kicked at him, but her sneakers made little impact.

He pulled the door closed and the van sped on, sending her rolling across the metal floor even as she continued to shove ineffectively at the large man. A second later, he'd covered her body with his, the way he might go after a fumbled football. The weight of him drove the air from her lungs, not that screaming would have done much good.

She swatted at his head, and for the first time realized that she knew him. He was one of van Winter's bodyguards. Before she could do anything else, a strange lethargy entered her body. Numbness immediately followed, then black circles danced before her eyes.

Struggling to focus, she thought she saw a needle in the man's hand, pulling back from her, but then her vision faded and she lost her hold on consciousness.

Chapter 19

Diego paced as Diana filled him in on what had happened just a few hours earlier.

Ryder sat beside her, along with Melissa Danvers and her husband, Sebastian. Diana obviously felt Ramona's absence was important enough to call this meeting at Ryder's apartment.

"Ramona was supposed to meet me at one o'clock for lunch. Right after her appointment with Melissa."

"One of my assistants, Sara Martinez, remembers seeing Ramona get on the elevator at around twelve-thirty," Melissa added.

"Time enough to get to the restaurant on foot. After waiting for half an hour, I tried calling her, but there was no answer," Diana said. "After that I raced to the hospital."

"But there was no sign of her?" Diego wondered aloud, in a way not surprised that no one had seen anything. New Yorkers set on their typical routines had a tendency to wear blinders.

"One of the hospital guards said a homeless man came into the lobby claiming that someone had been grabbed on the corner," Melissa said, worry evident in her tone. "We have to find her. She needs to take her medications."

"Why didn't the guard alert the police?" Diego asked.

Diana shook her head. "After mentioning the kidnapping, the homeless man went on to say the Men in Black had done it so that no one would know it had been an alien."

Diego raked back his locks and blew out a frustrated sigh before venting his anger on her. "Why did you let her run around alone, anyway?"

Ryder seemed ready to come to her defense, but Diana laid a gentling hand on his thigh. "Ramona insisted. She thought it would be better for me to spend my time investigating rather than babysitting. Hard to argue with that logic."

"Except now she's missing," he nearly shouted. Fear was gripping him, hard. Esperanza had been gone for several hours, as well, before they had realized she'd been taken. They hadn't discovered her whereabouts until it was too late.

He didn't want to lose Ramona like that, too. His desire to save her went way beyond the promise he had made to help her. In the past few days without her, his life had been bleak, lonely. In the short time they had been together, she had made an irrefutable impact on his life. He wasn't sure he wanted to go back to the way his life had been before she'd come into it.

But finding her wouldn't change that. She was human and she was dying. Only one thing could alter the ultimate outcome of that linear human existence.

Ryder's voice interrupted Diego's musing, and he looked up. The other vampire's face mirrored his own emotions. The want. The despair. The love.

Diego realized he was in love with Ramona, much as he might try to deny it. But he couldn't allow that emotional morass to cloud his mind right now. He would deal with her mortality when the time came. "We need to find her, and fast," he declared.

"Definitely. Her system is too compromised to be without her medications for any length of time," Melissa reiterated.

"Her phone is still on, so I can try to track it. That is, if it's with her and wasn't dropped somewhere along the way," Sebastian said. With his hacker skills, he would be able to use his computer to get some information on her whereabouts.

"Hopefully the GPS chip is enabled. Can you do it from here?" Diana asked, inclining her head in the direction of Ryder's home office.

"Better I go to our apartment. My equipment's got more bells and whistles," her brother explained, and with a parting kiss on his wife's forehead, left the room.

"What if we can't track it?" Diego asked, and began pacing again, thinking about whether any of his vamp abilities would be of use, not that they had helped to save Esperanza. Smells would carry only so far, and Ramona's mortality meant she wasn't as traceable as one of his vamp friends, whose power and presence he could sometimes sense from quite a distance.

Diana rose from the couch, stood in his path and laid a hand on his chest. "We have options. I've got some other developments, but I need you to calm down."

Balling his fists, he loomed over her petite form, almost glowering as he said, "Tell us what you've got, because right now I'm all for flying over to van Winter's place and tearing him apart until I get an answer."

"Which would accomplish nothing. We need to get the goods on van Winter to clear Ramona. To keep her from going to jail," the agent explained.

"Ramona says she didn't sign the copies. Will the pictures I took help prove that?"

"I've got a friend in handwriting analysis who said he would compare the signatures. The problem is, if Ramona didn't sign them, who did?"

"It could have been Luis Rodriguez or even van

Winter himself," Ryder suggested. "There were probably few people who had access."

Diana nodded. "I'll try to get samples of their handwriting for additional comparison."

Reining in the demon who would willingly inflict punishment to meet his needs, Diego stepped back. "What other information do you have?"

From the coffee table Diana picked up an envelope she'd tossed there earlier. She pulled out a series of photos.

"John Henry, nicknamed Big John. He's got several priors."

Something niggled in Diego's mind about the man in the mug shots and he struggled to recall where he had seen the face before.

"He's familiar to you?" Diana asked, reading his body language.

"He is," Diego admitted, and as he flipped from one set of mug shots to the next, he realized where he had seen the man. "I think this is one of van Winter's bodyguards. He was at the gallery the day of the show."

He pointed to a later photo of the felon, where he carried a little more weight than in the earlier ones. If memory served Diego correctly, the man was even stockier now. "His face is heavier, and he's thicker through the chest and arms."

Diego flinched as he looked at the notations on the various rap sheets, which detailed a long history of arrests for violent crimes. "Why would van Winter hire a goon like this?"

"To do his dirty work," Diana replied, easing the photos from his hands. "I suspect he's the one who grabbed Ramona. The hospital promised us access to the feeds from the outside security cameras. Hopefully, they got a good glimpse of him."

"And you'll be able to do something with all this?" Diego asked.

She hesitated, and at that delay, Ryder finally piped in. "Can you do anything, given your current duty assignment?"

Diego remembered Ryder's comments some time ago about Diana being on desk duty. He suspected that meant she shouldn't be involved in any kind of investigation. "Diana?" he pressed, anxious to hear her answer.

"I'll talk to the assistant director. I'll explain the urgency of the situation. With a little more information we may be able to convince a judge to issue a search warrant."

"And what if we can't get more info?" Diego challenged.

"If we get the video segments shortly, we may have a shot of the abduction, and if Sebastian can triangulate her location—"

"That's a lot of ifs." His common sense told him Diana had to build a case that would hold up before a judge. His vampire sense, however, only understood action. It didn't want to wait for pieces of paper when there were more effective ways to secure what he wanted.

Diana seemed to sense his mood, and as he started past her, she pressed her hand against his chest. Despite her small size, she was strong. Maybe a little too strong for a mortal. As he met her gaze, she quickly pulled back, as if realizing she had given away something. Despite that, she urged, "Don't do anything crazy. If we don't have enough by morning—"

Melissa jumped into the discussion. "You can't let it go too long. We've stabilized her with the latest medications, but if she's off them for even a short while, there could be complications."

"Like what?" Diego asked curtly, wanting to understand in the event that—

Banishing that image, he listened patiently as Melissa explained about Ramona's anemia, how they had determined it was an autoimmune reaction, and what her body might do to itself if she wasn't properly medicated.

After she had finished, he looked around the room at all of them. Friends one and all, who had always been by his side. He hoped they would be this time, as well.

"I'm not going to let her die while some judge decides if there's enough paperwork on his desk. If you don't know by tomorrow, I'll deal with van Winter myself."

* * *

Her eyes were heavy-lidded as she tried to wake. Her limbs were leaden and sore. With a shake of her head, Ramona tried to drive away the cobwebs that had spun themselves around her brain. It only succeeded in creating whirling images in her vision, which, when combined with the thick smell of gasoline in the small space, made her retch. As the dry heaves racked her body, her sides ached, prompting memories of being tackled by van Winter's bodyguard.

She realized she was strapped to a hard metal chair, her wrists bound behind her back, the bindings painfully tight. Thick rope wrapped around her upper body, loose enough to let her move a bit, but not work her way free.

Exhaustion had settled in, but she managed to lift her head. Her eyes slowly focused and she started to make out her surroundings.

The barest of light spilled in from behind her, but she couldn't turn enough to see where it came from. Before her and to the side were what looked like the doors of a truck. When she banged with her sneakered feet, the dull thud sounded metallic.

Gasoline vapors continued to permeate the stuffy space, and the heat seemed to increase the longer she sat there.

Ramona realized she was probably still in the van she had been thrown into earlier. She wondered why her kidnappers hadn't moved her somewhere else, but then again, killing her here would make it easier to dispose of her body and not dirty any of van Winter's precious belongings.

She had no doubt that's what they intended to do, much like they had killed poor Luis Rodriguez. She wondered why they hadn't done it already.

The minutes ticked by slowly and she sat there, her body a combination of numbness from the inactivity and pain from the physical attack earlier that day. She hadn't thought herself claustrophobic, but as time passed, it seemed harder to breathe in the stale, hot, petroleum-scented air.

Sweat oozed from her body, soaking her clothes and adding to her discomfort as, little by little, a chill began in her center and spread outward.

She recognized the signs. She knew her body was getting weaker from the absence of the medicines that kept her going. As the coldness spread, a pain racked her head, its angry tendrils reaching outward, taking hold in her skull.

Someone finally opened the side door of the van, illuminating the space. She flinched from the light, but forced herself to keep her eyes on the arrivals—van Winter and his bodyguard.

"Good evening, Ramona. I trust we haven't inconvenienced you too much," the older man said as he stepped into the vehicle.

His bodyguard followed, hunching his tall body despite the relative spaciousness of the interior. He opened a folding chair for the multimillionaire and then another for himself. Once they were both seated, the bodyguard shut the door and snapped on a dome light.

"What do you want?" she asked, gritting her teeth as her voice echoed through her skull.

"Alicia Tipton called to thank me for allowing such a marvelous work to leave my collection. She mentioned that Diego Rivera had come by," van Winter said.

"That's not surprising, since Mrs. Tipton paid a nice sum for one of my latest works." Truthful, but Ramona suspected Diego's visit had had nothing to do with the canvas Alicia had purchased.

Van Winter inclined his head in the direction of the bodyguard, who rose and hunched beside her. She refused to flinch. Instead, she lifted her chin and shot the thug a look that she hoped seemed more annoyed than scared.

"We can do this in one of two ways, Ramona. One is, you tell me who you've spoken to and what you've told them. Two, I let Big John convince you to tell me." Van Winter crossed his legs and straightened the pleat on his pants, as fastidious as always.

"So you can do to them what you did to Luis?" she retorted straining forward against the rope.

Big John jerked toward her, fist raised. She did what she didn't want to do—she flinched. But then she immediately glared at him to make up for it. "You don't scare me."

The bodyguard menaced her again, but van

Winter called him off. "Not yet, John. You can have your fun with her later, after we've talked."

"I'm not talking." She relaxed in her chair and took a breath as the headache that had been taking root blossomed in her skull until it felt as if her head would explode.

"Not feeling well, my dear?" van Winter asked.

But she couldn't respond. She couldn't do anything but hold her breath and hope the pain would pass. The pressure built until, like water bursting through a dam, blood rushed from her nose and ran over her lips and chin.

She tipped her head back, hoping to stem the flow. Instead, the blood leaked down the back of her throat. The sharp copper taste filled her mouth. She wondered for a moment if this was what Diego hungered for. If this was what he dreamed of at night.

"Boss, what should I do?" Big John asked, but van Winter only chuckled.

"This is rather beneficial, actually. She'll die all on her own. We won't have to go through the bother of doing anything other than dumping her body somewhere."

The blood dripping down her throat made her choke. She leaned forward and coughed, sending blood and saliva flying from her mouth and onto van Winter's shoes and pant legs.

"We can help you feel better," he said as he withdrew a handkerchief from his breast pocket and dabbed it away.

Her head lolled forward, feeling heavier than it had before. The nosebleed was draining her, as was the headache. Her midday dose of pills might help stop both, but she knew the price would be high.

"I need my medicine. It's in my apartment." Her voice sounded weak and she sagged against the restraints.

Big John looked to van Winter, but the old man waved him off. "We can't afford to be seen around her place."

Big John placed his thumb and forefinger on her chin, picking up her head until she stared at his brutish face. "Be nice. Talk to us."

Talk to them and have them go after her friends? After Diego? She shook her head, or at least thought she did.

"The medicines for some names," the body-guard teased.

"Let it go. Maybe if she's suffering enough, she'll reconsider and tell us what she knows." Van Winter rose then and Big John leaped into action, opening the door for him and then closing it once again, sealing himself alone with her inside the back of the van.

Roughly he grasped her chin and jerked her head up once more. "Don't be stupid. The boss man means business."

"Water," she said, her voice a tiny croak as she tried to swallow.

"Don't have any. Blood will have to do." Before she could ask again, he left the van, securely shutting the panel door behind him and plunging her into darkness once again.

She knew her body well enough to know she was in a bad way. She wondered how much longer she could last if she didn't get her medicines.

Closing her eyes, she willed herself to rest, praying as she did so that her friends would find her in time.

That she'd be able to say goodbye to Diego.

Chapter 20

Diego sat beside Sebastian as he played the video feeds from the security cameras trained on the streets around the hospital.

The first two tapes yielded little, as they were of the west and north and Ramona had exited out the east, according to the hospital security guard.

The third feed provided a glimpse of her leaving through the revolving doors, a broad smile on her face. Diego's heart sped up at the radiance of that smile, but a second later, they lost sight of her as she walked southward. The time on the video indicated that it had been twelve thirty-five.

He sneaked a quick peek at his watch. It was nearly seven now. Melissa didn't know whether

Ramona had her medications with her and even if she did, he knew van Winter wouldn't care about making sure she got them. It would be way too convenient for him if Ramona died from her illness instead of a suspicious hit-and-run like the one that had killed his former employee.

The last video captured the southern side of the building, and Sebastian immediately advanced to the proper time frame. As expected, Ramona came into view and the wide camera lens tracked her passage into the crosswalk. At that point the real action began.

An unmarked white delivery truck jerked to a halt before Ramona. From behind her, a large, muscular man grabbed her and tossed her into it, then jumped in himself before the van sped away.

Sebastian returned to the start of the segment. He pushed a number of buttons on the computer. "I'm making a copy you can take to Diana."

His sister had returned to her office in the hopes that her experts would have more information for her. She had agreed that if Sebastian was able to get anything on the cell phone or from the videos, either Diego or Ryder would run it down to her.

Sebastian again rewound the video and went about enlarging and enhancing key images. By the time he finished, Diego had a clear picture of the man who had grabbed Ramona—none other than Big John Henry—and the plate number from the van.

Fingers flying over the keys, Sebastian said,

"I'm loading these images onto the thumb drive for Diana and e-mailing them. I'm also printing them out. I'll call her in a second with the plate number."

The laser printer by his side flashed to life and a moment later, Sebastian placed the photos and USB drive in an envelope for his sister. "Tell her I'm sorry I couldn't triangulate the cell phone signal," he said as he handed Diego the envelope. "It was just too weak."

With a nod, Diego went into the living room, where Ryder sat with Melissa. "I'm heading out," he said, holding up the envelope and drawing their attention.

"I can go with you," Ryder offered.

"Not without me," Melissa stated. "If Ramona needs medical attention, I'm the one she'll need."

Although Melissa was correct, having her along would only slow things down, and Diego didn't want to waste a minute in getting the information to Diana. "Why don't you wait here with Ryder? As soon as we can move on van Winter, we'll call you."

She didn't argue, but as Diego walked toward the French doors leading out to the balcony, Ryder rose and followed him. Once outside, they walked to the low wall enclosing the garden.

Ryder clapped him on the back. "Do you know what you will do once you find her?"

Diego faced his friend. The moonlight played across Ryder's features, glistening in his dark hair and eyes. His mouth was a harsh slash across his face. "We'll get her to a hospital."

"And then? What if that's not enough?"

Diego considered the many centuries he had been undead. The countless humans who had come and gone—and the many vampires. Those vamps who had "gone" had possibly made a bigger impression on him than the humans. There had been those chased down by self-styled slayers and hunters. Those driven mad by their eternal lives, who had chosen to end their existence with a walk into the sun or fire, or a carefully planned beheading—sometimes self-inflicted. Then there was the worst he had seen—a vampire who had downed a bottle of holy water and suffered for days as the water ate at his insides like acid in a human.

Maybe reaching the status of elder ranked even higher on the list of why Diego hesitated to consider turning Ramona. The elders were the worst of everything vampire. Lacking any trace of humanity, they satisfied their hungers and expressed their angers without a qualm. Only a few, like his friend Stacia, somehow managed to hold on to any kindness, but even then, it came with a price.

In a few short centuries Diego would be an elder. He already ranked highly within the local vamp hierarchy. Would he lose his humanity like the others?

And if he did, what about Ramona? Could she deal with eternal life or would it change her? Would it sluggishly strangle the emotions that had come to life between them and bring them eternal regret?

"Diego?" Ryder pressed at his prolonged silence.

He spread his arms wide to the city stretching out before them. "See all this, *amigo?* I remember when the el used to clank up Third Avenue and horse carriages brought the Fifth Avenue elite to their town homes."

"Things change."

"People change as well. Esperanza did. Even I've changed, and maybe not for the better." He dropped his hands to his sides. "I'm not sure I could handle eternal life if Ramona changed for the worse. If I killed the passion that beats in her heart."

"It's a heart that will be forever stilled if you do nothing. If you cannot take a chance that all the goodness in that heart will survive."

"Is that what you tell yourself, Ryder, as you lie beside Diana? You deceive yourself." He shot a look at him from the corner of his eye and realized he had ripped deep into his friend's heart. But he couldn't apologize. Not when Ryder wasn't being truthful with either of them.

"I must go," Diego said. He surged up onto the ledge and transformed. When the vampire emerged, he sped off, a blur in the dark of the night.

The glare of the light as the van door opened roused Ramona. Barely. The pain in her head had spread to other parts of her body. Her joints and abdomen. Something warm wet her lips again. Another trickle of blood from her nose.

She stared at Big John when he stepped in, but his image wavered as dizziness assailed her.

"Boss man will be here in a few minutes. He suggested I go ahead and convince you to talk," he said as he positioned himself in front of her.

"I'm not afraid of you."

"Little girl, I can make your last moments very unpleasant." To prove his point, he stepped behind her and grabbed hold of her bound wrists, pulling them upward.

Her arms screamed in agony, but she bit her lip to keep from crying out. She wouldn't give him the satisfaction.

He jerked again and leaned over her shoulder, bringing his mouth close to her ear. Softly he said, "Maybe it's not pain that'll make you talk. Maybe you need something else."

Dropping her hands, Big John reached from behind and groped her breast, his big hand squeezing painfully.

"That's enough," van Winter commanded as he came to the door.

Big John immediately left her to help van Winter up into the vehicle. The old man had changed into evening wear, clearly ready for a night out. As he had before, he settled himself on the chair and crossed his legs.

"I don't have time for games, Ramona. My

presence is demanded at a dinner honoring my various charitable donations."

"Sucks for you," she said, and Big John slapped her across the face.

Her head snapped back and she tasted fresh blood from where she had bitten the inside of her cheek. She struggled for breath, her chest suddenly tight. After a few quick, shallow inhalations, she managed to say, "Thought you were going to let Mother Nature take care of me."

"Oh, she will, but a few bruises here and there are easily explained by a fall. Tell me who you told about poor Luis. And why was Rivera so eager to visit Alicia Tipton's collection?"

Her chest rose and fell with difficulty, each breath harder to take. "You had someone sign the copies. Who? Luis?"

Van Winter chuckled harshly. "Luis could barely sign his own name."

"Then who?" she asked, focusing on the thin, angular lines on his face, and as she did so, it came to her. "You did it."

The smugness that had been on his visage faded immediately. "This is your last chance."

"I'm a dead woman regardless of what I say, but understand this—Diego knows nothing. I've told no one."

"Rather unbelievable, my dear, and so you leave me no choice." He gestured to Big John. "Go pick up Rivera."

* * *

Diana accepted the envelope from Diego, looked at the photos and combined them with the other papers on her desk. She calmly tucked them into the folder.

"What do we do now?" he asked, unnerved by her quiet.

"*We* don't do anything. *I'm* going to see my assistant director." She rounded her desk, intending to leave her office, but Diego grabbed her arm as she went by.

"*We* are going to see your director."

"That's not SOP, Diego." She met his gaze, her own defiant, but he was not about to back down.

"I don't even care what SOP means. Let's go."

She clearly resented his insistence. Despite that, she nodded curtly and ripped her arm from his grasp, once again surprising him with her strength as she stalked out of the office.

He was hot on her heels and nearly bowled her over when she stopped abruptly at one door. Entering, he realized they were in a large anteroom. The door to the office beyond was open and a handsome Latino sat in a leather executive chair, his head bent as he pored over the papers on his desk.

Diana walked to the door and knocked.

He looked up and appeared confused for a millisecond before he smiled. "Come in, Diana."

"*Gracias,* Jesus. This is Diego Rivera," she said, motioning to him.

Diego held out his hand and the other man rose, shook it and introduced himself. "Jesus Hernandez, Assistant Director in Charge."

"Thank you for taking the time to meet with us," Diego murmured.

"Is that what I'm doing?" he asked, arching an eyebrow, though his look and tone were friendly.

"Jesus, I need to ask for a search warrant," Diana said, and handed him the file.

The earlier good humor on the man's face fled with her request. Without another word, he sat in his chair and reviewed the papers she had assembled. With each sheet he flipped, his manner became more abrupt, until he reached the last item and slammed the file shut.

"Please tell me you didn't work on this case," the ADIC said, glaring at Diana as he did so.

"Diego and Ramona are my friends. I couldn't—"

"You deliberately defied the review board. At a minimum—"

"A woman's life is at stake," Diana pleaded, but Jesus continued as if uninterrupted.

"They will extend your suspension from active duty. At worst—"

"They'll ask for my resignation. I'll gladly give it if I can save Ramona's life." Diana reached for the file on his desk and opened it again. "This is a solid case," she urged. "We've got van Winter's bodyguard on video doing the snatch, and his prints on threatening photos."

Jesus closed the file. "Frederick van Winter is one of the most powerful and influential men in the country, and from all appearances, Ramona Escobar is a forger."

Diego jumped to her defense. "Ramona did not commit forgery."

Diana laid a hand on his arm. "Look again, Jesus," she said, and gestured to the file.

He did as she asked, and his eyes widened while reviewing one piece of paper. When he put it down, he said, "Our experts peg van Winter as the one who put the signatures on the paintings?"

Nodding, Diana said, "There were undeniable characteristics between van Winter's signature and those on the masterpieces sold at auction."

Closing the file, Jesus handed it back to her and said, "We'll have to get a warrant."

"There's got to be some way to expedite this. Her life is at risk without her medications," Diego interjected but the ADIC was already on the phone to a judge.

After, he motioned to Diana. "Finish this tonight. Tomorrow I'll have to bring your actions before the review board."

The agent rose from her chair. "*Gracias,* Jesus. I'll need backup—"

"Take Maggie Gonzalez. I think she's still down in the lab. Her medical expertise should help, as well. After you've got the warrant, call NYPD and put out an APB on the van and the two suspects. Also ask for some uniforms to secure the scene."

"Will do," she said, and headed out the door.

Diego lingered, shifting from foot to foot, torn up about the assistant director's comments. "Diana did the right thing by helping us."

"I expect my agents to follow the rules. If they don't, I'd have bedlam in here." Shaking his head in disgust, Jesus added, "Good luck finding your friend."

Chapter 21

Not even the Inquisitor had inflicted the kind of torture visited on Diego as he sat outside the judge's chambers, waiting for him to issue a decision on the warrant Diana had requested. Beside Diego sat the attractive doctor that Jesus Hernandez had named as Diana's backup.

Dr. Maggie Gonzalez had a model's long build, enhanced with the kinds of curves a woman should have. Her remarkable green eyes were filled with intelligence, and thick auburn hair framed her striking features.

Though she was the kind of woman a man couldn't fail to notice, Diego's only interest in her centered on whether she could help find Ramona.

The door to the judge's chambers opened and Diana walked out. "I've got it. Let's go."

Diego would have preferred to use his vampire speed. Instead he had to climb into the backseat of a standard issue, late-model sedan and endure the delays. Even with the siren and lights, they battled traffic heading uptown. As Maggie drove, Diana called a contact at the police department, ordered the APBs and requested uniformed backup.

Although it took less than twenty minutes to make the trip, it seemed forever. When they finally arrived at the van Winter building on Sixth, two police cars were waiting there, along with some familiar faces.

Ryder and Melissa stood on the sidewalk with the uniformed officers, plus Detective Peter Daly, an old friend who could be trusted to guard their secrets.

After Maggie pulled the sedan behind the police cars, they exited and met up with the detective and uniforms. Daly was the first to speak.

"I hope you know what you're doing, Diana. Van Winter's attorneys are already here," Daley explained. "He called them from the charity event he was attending when one of my partners went to fetch him."

"We need to get inside and search as quickly as possible. A woman's life is at stake," Diana informed the detective.

"First hurdle's going to be the suits. They're waiting for us by the front door." Daly gestured to the building set a distance back from the avenue. The glass encircling the entire lower floor provided a clear view of two men in business suits and a cadre of four or five security guards.

"Let's go, then," she said. But as Diego went to follow, Diana stopped him. "No civilians."

Melissa protested first. "She's going to need medical attention. I stopped by the hospital earlier to get some supplies."

Diego noticed she held a medical bag in one hand, along with a cooler labeled with a biohazardous sign. Blood, he suspected.

Maggie Gonzalez stepped forward. "Give it to me. Once we find her, we'll call for you to meet us."

Melissa handed over the cooler, reluctant but aware that time spent arguing was time wasted.

Diana shot Ryder and Diego an anxious look. "You know what I need to do. The main thing is to preserve the crime scene so we can nail the old bastard."

"Let's get moving, Di," Daly said, and as they walked away, he called the uniformed officers to go with them.

Diego watched them. At the door to the building, they met resistance just as Daly had expected. Diego itched to go over and burst through the phalanx of security guards blocking the way. He hadn't even realized he'd made a motion in that direction until Ryder's arm swept across his chest, holding him in place.

"Easy, *amigo*. Diana knows what she's doing."

Diego watched as she handed one of the suited men the warrant and they conversed. Her hands were braced on her hips, her posture confident. With a wave of her hand, she managed to part the sea of security guards, and her people moved forward toward the elevators.

"How long will it be now?" he wondered aloud, glancing up at the metal-and-glass building. Where in all that coldness had van Winter hidden Ramona? He didn't want to consider the possibility that she wasn't there.

Ryder followed his gaze, and once the majority of people had cleared out of the lobby, his friend said, "Race you up."

Confusion reigned for a moment as Diego scanned the fifty or more stories to the uppermost floor and van Winter's penthouse. The sheer glass walls would make the climb impossible and there were no buildings nearby to provide a launch point for accessing the penthouse, unless…

The older buildings on Seventh were not as tall, but their rooftops would be easier to access. A strong enough leap might get them to their target.

"Let's go," he said, but Melissa protested.

"Diana said—"

"That we needed to preserve the crime scene. She meant that we should look but not touch," Ryder explained.

Melissa nodded as if realizing that with their

powers, Ryder and Diego might have one up on the humans searching the scene. "Call me as soon as you know anything."

"The same," Ryder said. At his nod, they sped off toward Seventh, moving so quickly that the few scattered pedestrians on the street likely sensed no more than a breeze as they passed by.

On the northwest corner of Seventh stood a small commercial building, barely more than four stories high, but it abutted a taller structure. Once on the roof of the first building, Diego paused beside Ryder and surveyed their possible options. A leap to the next building's roof and then a dash up the fire escape on another would put them within ten stories of the penthouse of the van Winter building across the street.

With a running start, Diego could make the leap, but could Ryder, who was younger and arguably not as strong? "Can you make it?" he asked, even as he was in motion, easily jumping the few stories to the rooftop of the adjacent building.

On that level, Ryder paused beside him, surveyed the distance across the avenue and upward. "I'm not sure."

"If we make the jump, will we be noticed?"

"It's clear for now," Ryder said, glancing toward the uppermost floor.

Diego was puzzled by his friend's certainty, until it occurred to him. "You can sense Diana and what she's thinking. You've bitten her often."

A flush of chagrin swept across his friend's face. "Yes, I can sense her at times, when she's not blocking me. She's gotten quite good at that."

It was a power that came with intimacy of the most intense kind between lower vamps. Elders possessed that ability solely due to their age. As Diego released the tight control he exerted over his own vampire abilities, he picked up sketchy images from Ryder's mind. Violent images, but not of vampire mayhem. Of human malevolence. Within him the connection blossomed and suddenly, much as he imagined it was with Stacia, the vision sharpened and he tapped into the emotions running rampant through his friend.

Diego was nearly undone by them all, so vividly alive. So achingly sad as he realized the truth of his friend's relationship. Of Diana's failing mortality.

Ryder could not make the leap, but it wasn't just about the jump to the next building. Ryder couldn't make the leap to turn Diana. Diego understood it well. The maelstrom of doubt and yearning was much like his own.

Snagging the back of Ryder's neck, he pulled him into a tight embrace and whispered, "I understand."

When they broke apart, Diego turned his face upward to the skyscraper that gleamed like silver in the moonlight. Ryder, however, looked downward. Diego glanced where his friend pointed—the entrance to the parking garage beneath the building.

In silent agreement, they separated. Ryder returned to the lower rooftop, dropped to the ground below and dashed across the street in a blur to human eyes, though Diego noted his passage easily.

When his friend had entered the parking garage, Diego moved to an edge of the rooftop and gauged the distance to the van Winter building. He summoned every ounce of his inhuman strength and raced back across the roof.

With a surge of power, he made the leap.

He flew upward, streamlining his body to avoid wind resistance. It occurred to him in midflight that this leap was about more than the chasm of the busy New York avenue below and the glass skyscraper before him.

It was a leap away from his vamp life as he had known it, and into the embrace of humanity with all its attendant pain and death. With all its emotion.

Whether it was love or blood that had called him, he'd be a fool to ignore the emotions Ramona roused in him.

The impact against the side of the building jarred the breath out of him, but he luckily found a hold in the metal window washers' channels between the glass panels. Taking a moment to collect himself after his less than graceful landing, Diego realized he was just a few feet below the penthouse level. Luckily again, the floor with which he had painfully connected was empty and dark. Nothing within or above hinted that his presence had been noted.

Down below might be a different story, he thought, wondering whether anyone would see him plastered there, fifty stories up. Maybe an eagle-eyed tourist with his trusty camera.

With that thought in mind, Diego braced his toes as best he could against the glass, dug into the metal channels with his fingers and heaved upward one last time. He managed to get himself over the ledge, and as he landed, rolled toward some tall, dark shapes along one side of the penthouse balcony.

Trees. A row of them in large pots created a barrier along one edge. He crouched behind one of the immense ceramic containers and peered toward the windows along one wall of the penthouse. With his heightened vamp senses, he could see past the glass to the figures who had entered and were once again arguing by the front door.

Closing his eyes, he focused on those muffled sounds until they sharpened and he could make out the discussion.

"The warrant is for the van Winter building, including any and all offices, residences or common areas owned, inhabited or frequented by one Frederick van Winter or John Henry," Diana calmly told the multimillionaire's attorneys. She didn't wait for a reply. "Fan out," she instructed her team.

Diego picked up the sounds of shoes scuffing

and tapping on the floors and carpets. The cops and two agents, their steps and sounds distinct. One approached the windows.

Diana, he realized, without even opening his eyes. He could sense her much like he could another vamp, which puzzled him until he recollected the scattered images he had picked up in Ryder's brain earlier. The fear that Diana was somehow different now.

The FBI agent spared but a moment to scope out the balcony before returning to her search, yet Diego got the feeling she knew he was there. She'd sensed him much like his vamp radar had registered her presence.

Long minutes passed torturously, and he couldn't wait there any longer, wondering what was happening inside.

He surged forward, toward another set of planters closer to the window, and positioned himself there, holding his breath as he noticed the two attorneys standing by the windows.

Had they heard or seen him?

When they remained inside, their attention clearly focused on the ongoing search, Diego relaxed and released a shaky breath. The sound of the penthouse door opening grabbed his attention. It was followed by the hurried steps of two men entering, then van Winter's angry voice.

"What is the meaning of this?" he asked as Diana met him in the space just before the windows.

She flashed her badge and was about to explain when Maggie Gonzalez stepped out of another room holding two plastic bags. From his position, Diego could make out what looked like a bundle of clothing and shoes.

"These were in a pile for cleaning," Maggie said. "They tested positive for blood."

Rage surged through Diego, breaking through the control he had on his demon. Instantly the fangs exploded from his mouth. He had to grip the edges of the pot before him to restrain himself. The pottery crumbled beneath his fingers as he fought the desire to tear van Winter apart.

The older man barely glanced at the bags and, with a carefree shrug, replied, "A slight accident I had this morning."

Diana took the bags from Maggie and examined the one with the clothing. With a shake of her head, she said, "You'll have to do better than that. These are high velocity blood spatters."

The man shrugged again. "I have nothing to say."

"Really?" Diana walked right up to him. "If Ramona Escobar dies because you don't talk, all the high-priced lawyers in the world aren't going to be enough to protect you."

Van Winter backed away from her, seemingly unfazed. "Is that a threat?"

"A promise," Diana said, and walked to one wall lined by light maple bookcases filled with an assortment of books, photos and art objects. Motioning to it, she said, "There's something not right about the spacing between these bookcases and the bedroom. There's too much dead space."

Daly stepped up from behind van Winter and examined the area. "I think you're right, Special Agent." He instructed two of his men to clear off the bookcases. To the other two he said, "See if you can get a sledgehammer, and if not, grab a battering ram from one of the cruisers."

"You can't do this," van Winter protested, finally beginning to lose his unnatural calm.

"I see now just how sick you are, Frederick. You have no care for humans, only for this." Diana gestured at all the appointments in the luxurious apartment.

Her words struck a little too close to home for Diego. At one time, he had been much like van Winter. But no longer. And he could no longer wait there, wondering about Ramona's whereabouts. He doubted she was in the space behind the bookcases. Van Winter would not be stupid enough to do that.

Which meant that she was either with his bodyguard or in some other part of the building. Or worse, he thought, somewhere not nearby at all.

Daly's cell phone rang. The detective answered, but the voice on the other end of the line was too muffled for Diego to discern.

"A patrol car spotted John Henry in Soho and grabbed him," Daly said when he clicked off.

A second later, Diana's cell phone chirped, as well, but Diego knew it was only a diversion. He had sensed a change in her as she stood there, and knew that Ryder had somehow communicated with her. She spoke briefly into the phone and afterward addressed the attorneys. "The warrant gives us permission to search all the common areas. Peter, can you get us a few more uniforms?"

"Will do. What's next?" Daly asked.

"Maggie, come with me. Let's check the lobby and any points of egress. Have the uniforms meet us there. We can fan out to the basement and common areas."

Diego knew just where she would instruct them to go—to the underground parking garage. He suspected Ryder had found something and had clued Diana in on it moments earlier.

Diego wasn't about to wait a second longer.

Chapter 22

A low, insistent thudding penetrated the fog she had slipped into. She imagined someone calling her name in rhythm with the pounding beats.

Ramona. Ramona. Ramona.

She tried to raise her head, but it lolled listlessly to the side. Her mouth bone-dry, she called out, but only managed a strangled croak.

The intensity of the pounding increased and she heard other muffled voices from beyond the metal door, followed by a loud bang and the shattering of glass.

"She's in here."

A moment later, a police officer was at her side,

his face fuzzy in her vision. "You're okay, miss. We'll get you free in a second."

He left her and opened the side door, allowing others into the small space.

She squinted against the brighter light, and as she did so, Diego's face came into focus. She mouthed his name, unable to phonate as her breath failed her.

"Easy, *querida.* Help is here." He knelt by her side as the police officers began removing the bindings.

When she sagged forward, Diego was there, catching her before she fell and taking her into his arms. She leaned into him and closed her eyes, feeling incredibly tired.

Diego sensed the thready and rapid beat of her heart as he grasped her and jumped down from the van. The indignant whine of the ambulance Diana had called echoed against the walls of the subbasement before the driver screeched to a halt beside the van and shut off the siren.

Diego carried her to the back of the ambulance, Diana and Maggie at his sides. He didn't wait for the EMTs to pull out the gurney; he hopped into the back of the ambulance and gently laid her on it. Maggie joined him, but asked him to step aside so that she could examine Ramona.

Knowing how weak she was, he complied, hopping back down to where Diana was busy barking orders into her cell phone. Daly stood beside her, along with Ryder. As they waited, he heard the squealing tires of another vehicle approaching.

The police car stopped a few yards away and Melissa Danvers burst from the backseat and ran toward them.

As she took note of Maggie inside the ambulance, she jumped up and went to the other doctor's assistance, saying, "We can't delay. We need to get her to the hospital."

Maggie raced to the back of the ambulance, gave them a pained look and closed the doors. Diego heard someone shout to the drivers to get moving, and they hit the siren and lights, accelerated up the ramp and out of view.

He stood there, silently staring at his friends. Finally, Diana reached out and said, "Go. I'll finish things here and we'll meet you at the hospital."

He nodded and walked away from the officers at the scene. After jogging slowly across the nearly deserted parking lot until he was out of sight, he warped into vamp velocity.

Ramona managed a weak smile as Melissa's face came into focus. The doctor was hooking up an IV, while another woman came close and offered her small sips of water. Ramona drank slowly, but even that was too much. The water had no sooner gone down than she was retching it back up. It splattered against the brilliant white sheets on the gurney, staining them pink with streaks of blood.

"She might be hemorrhaging internally," the woman said, even as she passed a soft piece of moist gauze across Ramona's lips, trying to ease her thirst.

"Abdomen's distended," Melissa noted. Though she applied the slightest pressure, it was enough to radiate pain throughout Ramona's midsection. She moaned and arched her back, crying out in agony.

"I think her spleen and liver have been compromised, Maggie," Melissa advised.

"Hurts," Ramona whispered.

"We know, hon," said the woman. Gently, Maggie wiped away the dried remnants of blood and spittle from Ramona's face. When she once again offered her a soaked piece of gauze, Ramona sucked on it, able to keep down the almost minuscule amount of water.

A sharp turn sent both doctors reeling against the gurney. The jarring movement brought Ramona more pain. Within her chest, her heart raced and seemed to skip a beat. She struggled for breath, her body suddenly numb in spots.

A second later, Maggie slipped an oxygen mask over her face while Melissa stuck a syringe into the IV. Ramona shook her head, wanting to shout that she didn't need to sleep. She didn't want the unnatural rest the medicines provided.

She fought for one breath after another, a wild

rhythm taking hold in her chest until everything blurred. Still she battled the dullness brought on by the medications, thinking that she would have time enough to sleep when she was dead.

Diego hung back from the entrance for incoming patients, knowing that his arrival before the ambulance would draw the attention of the FBI agent with Melissa. While she appeared to be a friend of Diana's, he was unsure whether she knew of his and Ryder's peculiar state.

The minutes seemed interminable until he finally picked up the wail of an ambulance. Counting on it being the one with Ramona, he felt everything within him jump to life.

As the sounds grew closer, two orderlies opened the emergency room door and a short brunette nurse stepped from inside, a stethoscope draped around her neck. She seemed impatient, pacing back and forth near the doorway, never noticing him as he lurked in the shadows beyond. The narrow alley with the hospital's refuse bins provided a perfect hiding place.

The cry of the siren grew louder and then stopped before reaching him. He wondered why and stepped from his spot. That was when the nurse saw him, still in his vamp mode, but she said nothing, nor did she run. Instead, she curtly nodded her head, as if unfazed by his unusual state.

The ambulance sped by him, and as the glare of

the red and white lights bathed him, he used that opportunity to morph back to his human form. He hoped the nurse might be convinced that all she'd seen was a trick of the lights.

As the ambulance pulled up to the curb, the nurse went to the back to open the door. The EMTs helped bring down the gurney holding Ramona.

Even from this distance Diego could see how pale and still she was. The grim looks on the faces of Melissa and Maggie did nothing to assuage his fears about Ramona's condition. He waited until they were wheeling her in through the doors and then approached, trying to make it appear as if he had just arrived.

The nurse he had seen earlier was getting a report from Melissa when he stepped inside the entryway. "Can we help you?" she asked, her eyes narrowed as she took in his altered appearance.

"Diego," Melissa called. And at that the nurse asked, "You know him?"

Maggie came to his defense. "He's with us. I'll stay with him until—"

"I'm going wherever Ramona is going," he said, his tone adamant.

Maggie took on an alarmed expression, but Melissa calmed her. "It's okay, Maggie. Why don't you go wait for Diana in the lobby while we run all the tests and get Ramona comfortable."

The FBI agent's gaze skittered to Diego, but then she did as Melissa asked. When Diego glanced at Melissa, however, he got the sense that her use of the word *comfortable* had been a euphemism.

"She's not going to die," he said, and walked to Ramona's side. He almost wished he hadn't gotten near. Up close it was impossible not to realize her poor state. Short, labored breaths barely registered from beneath the oxygen mask covering her face. Her heartbeats were shallow, and as he placed a hand on her arm, the chill of her skin said death had taken root there.

"We need to get her to Intensive Care and start transfusions and medications," Melissa explained. With that, the nurse beside her waved to two orderlies waiting just beyond another set of doors. They quickly opened them and took over wheeling the gurney.

Melissa and the nurse followed, the young woman filling in Melissa on what she had prepped.

Diego lagged behind, wanting to stay out of their way so that they could do their work. When they got Ramona settled in Intensive Care, he watched them put a variety of different IVs into her arms and hand. After that, they swapped the portable oxygen bottle for a ventilator, wiring Ramona up to that machine as well as an assortment of other monitors.

When they finished, she seemed even more diminished in the tangle of wires and tubes running in and out of her body.

Before leaving, Melissa instructed the nurse to take a couple of vials of blood so they could run some tests. It was only then, when she had done all she could, that Melissa stepped to his side.

She spoke softly, her attention half on Ramona and half on a spot on the curtain behind him. She couldn't meet his gaze, which was not a good thing. "I'm worried that some of her organs have begun to fail. The transfusions may help stabilize her and keep her from going into total system failure. We're also giving her platelets and medications to curb some internal hemorrhaging."

Melissa didn't say it outright, but the message came across clearly. "How much longer does she have?"

With a shrug, the young doctor said, "No more than a few hours, if what we're doing now doesn't work."

His gut burned and his heart clenched in his chest. Sucking in a rough breath, he said, "Can you give us some time alone?"

Melissa nodded and motioned to the nurse, who walked over and introduced herself. "I'm Sara. I'll be staying on call as long as Ramona needs me."

"Thank you." He turned from them and walked to Ramona's side. He took her cold, limp hand, sandwiched it between his. Bending, he kissed her forehead, but no sign of awareness came with his actions.

Melissa eased a chair over to him and with a grateful nod, he moved it to the bedside. Once again his hands wrapped around Ramona's. He released his control on the vampire to give her warmth, and closed his eyes, but maybe it was better that he hadn't. The beast recognized Ramona's fragile hold on life. The heart that pumped too fast in a failing effort to support her body. The shallow, rapid breaths that accomplished little.

Bringing her hand to his lips, Diego whispered, "Please don't leave me."

Even though their time together had been short, he couldn't fathom life without her any more than he could imagine turning her. But those were the only choices now—let her die or make her undead.

Those words repeated in his brain like a litany while he sat by her side, hoping for some sign of improvement. But if anything, each visit by either Sara or Melissa only confirmed the beast's earlier diagnosis. It had been a couple of hours since they had brought her here, but her condition had barely improved. If anything, the steady drop of her vital signs in the monitors foretold what would happen.

Sara came in and set up another round of blood and liquids, her movements brisk and efficient. But as her gaze caught his, the tears glistening in her eyes were impossible to miss.

He didn't know how long it was after that when Ramona's hand twitched in his. He jumped up and leaned toward her. Her eyelids fluttered open and a pained smile came to her face.

His name slipped from her lips and she tightened her hold on his hand.

"I'm here, *amor,*" he said, and she murmured something else, too weak for him to hear even with the trace of vamp power he had released. He bent closer and this time the words were clear.

"Take me home."

"Take you home?" he repeated, thinking that if he took her away from all the equipment, she would…

"I want to die at home," she said, louder and with unwavering conviction.

He met her gaze and touched her cheek, hoping to dissuade her, but she reached up, removed the oxygen mask, and once again made her plea. "I want to die at home. In my own bed. In your arms."

Dios, why had she added the last, the one request he couldn't refuse?

With a nod, he said, "I'll go tell Melissa."

Chapter 23

Diego must have sensed her urgency and communicated it to the others, because they wasted no time in disconnecting her from the various monitors and IVs.

She struggled to hold on to consciousness, but it faded in and out like a television with a bad antenna, leaving her hearing only snatches of conversations. The one thing that stayed steady was Diego. He remained at her side, his hand holding hers.

A cold hand, which would warm on occasion. A vampire hand, her brain reminded her, not that she cared. She had seen the cruelty of humans, and Diego had been nothing but kind to her, so who were truly the monsters?

A cocoon of warmth surrounded her, and she heard a crinkling sound. A space blanket. She remembered it from the past, when they'd wrapped her in one to conserve her body heat. Then came the rock-solid strength of Diego's arms, lifting her and bringing her tight to his chest.

She opened her eyes and smiled, comforted by the security of his embrace. He forced a smile and bent until his lips brushed against hers. He whispered, "Hold on tight."

They were moving. Rapidly. A slight breeze washed over her and the world sped by, a blur of sights and sounds, with only one constant—Diego. His arms held her safely as he rushed her home, and she let herself go.

The hard strength of his arms receded, replaced by the familiar softness of her bed.

"No," she protested, and gripped his wrist.

"I'm not going anywhere, *querida,*" Diego said. Gently he eased her beneath the welcoming warmth of the covers, but it wasn't enough. With the absence of his embrace, her body began to tremble.

"Cold," she said.

He tucked the space blanket more tightly around her.

She wanted more. "Hold me."

The tremors racked her body and her skin took on an unnatural shade of white, nearly bloodless. Diego thought about slipping in beside her and holding her close, but his undead body lacked any heat in this form. As a vampire, however…

"Don't be afraid of me." He slowly morphed, allowing his demon form to emerge, and with it, the heat of the transformation.

She watched, fascinated instead of fearful, he realized. Cautious, he stopped halfway, leaving himself in a state half human, half vamp. He undid the buttons on his shirt, kicked off his shoes and eased under the covers. Shifting to her side, he tenderly slid his arm beneath her head, pillowing it, and brought his upper body close, hoping the warmth would help.

Gently he reached for the covers to pull them over both of them, but as he did so he brushed her midsection. She moaned and her body jerked with pain.

"I'm sorry," he said, but finished drawing up the thick bedspread and creating a haven of warmth for her.

Ramona snuggled near, the heat of his body providing solace. Besides the tenderness that brought agony with every touch, there was cold. Bone-deep cold that he helped to assuage with his presence.

But his proximity was about more than just his body heat. As she examined his dear face, she noticed the differences with the vampire awakened. His ice-blue eyes were an even brighter shade of blue, with hints of neon-green. Beneath his full upper lip the bump of fang was visible, and she reached up, traced his lip and then downward, to the sharp points.

She remembered his state the other night. This one was different. More human. More like the man she had come to love. With that thought came the recollection of the painting sitting across the loft, half finished. Raising her head, she peered toward it.

Moonlight illuminated the canvas where it sat on the easel. "I didn't get to finish it," she whispered, before dropping back down, her heart racing and her breath short from just that minor exertion.

As much as she tried to catch her breath, however, she couldn't. The cold and pain in her midsection grew. With her breath rasping in and out roughly, she fought to keep control, but it was too much. She moaned and tears came to her eyes as she said, "It hurts."

Diego gently brushed away a tear and cupped her face. "I know, *amor.* I know," he said, recalling the agony his own body had suffered while he waited for death at the hands of the Inquisitor.

Her breath exploded from her and she arched up off the bed. He could hear her madly beating heart and the rush of blood spilling wildly throughout her body as the hemorrhaging increased. It wouldn't be long now, he knew, and he tightened his embrace. There wasn't anything but pain filling her consciousness now.

Her hands gripped him, harder than he would have thought possible, and he heard her whispered plea. "Make it stop hurting."

He cupped her face and wiped away her tears. Her features shimmered as tears filled his own eyes. "I can't, love, but…stay with me. I want you to stay with me."

"I don't want to leave you. We haven't had enough time together."

"Are you sure, love?" he asked, maybe because he still needed to be convinced about the rightness of what he was considering.

"I've never been more sure of anything," she said, and brushed a kiss against his lips.

After, she bared her neck, but even as he bent his head toward her and fully released the vampire, he realized she might already be too far gone.

"Forgive me, *amor*. It will only hurt for a bit," he said, and with that, he sank his fangs deep into her neck and fed.

Her blood was powerless, offering little energy or rush, a testament to how debilitated she was physically. He barely drank from her for she was so close to death that he feared killing her himself. As he pulled away, her blood staining his lips and fangs, he realized how tenuous her grasp was on consciousness. He couldn't delay.

Raising his arm, he ripped open his wrist with his fangs and brought the bloody flesh to her mouth. She jerked her head away, but he urged her on. "Drink, *querida.* You need my blood to stay with me."

When he brought his wrist to her lips once again, she placed her mouth there and sucked. She licked at the blood oozing from his wrist, and her feeding stoked his vampire passion.

The animal wanted to feed from her again, but he knew to do so would bring certain death. He curbed the desire and patiently waited until her mouth stopped pulling at the wound, which healed almost instantly.

Her eyes were glazed as she looked up at him. "Sleep," he said. "You need to rest so my blood can restore you."

With a barely perceptible nod, she dropped off, and he lay down beside her, searching for any signs that the vampire's kiss had taken hold. Time passed and the familiar fever that came with a turning failed to appear.

Her heart still beat rapidly and weakly. Her breath was close to nonexistent, and she wouldn't rouse at his urging.

She would die, he thought, even with his turning her. Grief nearly overwhelmed him, until he realized he had to try again. He couldn't lose her.

He slashed his wrist once more and brought it to her mouth, but her lips remained slack. He settled for letting the blood drip into her mouth, and eventually she swallowed.

He repeated the feedings off and on all night

long, until the morning brought a knock at the door. Slipping from her side, he tossed on his shirt and answered it, finding Diana and Ryder on the threshold.

Diana looked ready to drop, her olive skin sallow, with deep, dark circles beneath her eyes. Ryder had his arm around her, as if she needed his support, and maybe she did. She was a bit unsteady as they entered.

"How is Ramona?" she asked, but Ryder seemed to immediately know.

"You turned her." The accusation was thick in his voice.

"Don't condemn me for something you wish you could do. For something you might have already started," he said, jerking his head in Diana's direction.

She shook her own head and laughed harshly. "Don't make assumptions, Diego. You don't know that."

"I feel it. I feel you. You're not human anymore." He was unprepared for the sadness that crept into her eyes and into those of her lover.

"Did she ask you to do it?" Ryder said.

"Yes, she did. I wouldn't have done so otherwise."

"How thoughtful of you." He sneered, but Diego cut him off with an angry slash of his hand.

"Enough. What happened with van Winter?" He had determined that if human justice failed, vamp vengeance would not.

"We found what appears to be the originals

behind a bookcase in his apartment. I think John Henry will testify in exchange for a lesser plea, but we're still working on that," Diana said.

"And Ramona? What about her part in it?" he asked, wondering what good it would do if she lived, if she had to spend her life behind bars.

"Van Winter is claiming that she was aware of what she was doing, and signed the paintings, but the evidence says otherwise. She may have to testify—"

"If she lives," he interrupted, and looked to where Ramona lay in bed, deathly still. "I'm not sure I turned her in time."

Ryder went to lay a hand on his shoulder, but Diego brushed it away. "Don't pity me. Or her. At least we were willing to take a chance at happiness."

"If you need anything, call," Diana said, and despite his earlier rebuff, she embraced Diego tightly.

He remained stiff in her arms for a second, but then relented, sensing the weakness in her body, but the determination in her heart.

"Thank you," he said, and she stepped back to Ryder's side.

They left and he returned to Ramona.

The transformation he had sown with his bite germinated later the next day.

He had struggled through a long, arduous night, cutting his wrists open time and time again to feed her. All during those long hours she had tenaciously clung to life, preserving hope within him.

When the sun began to rise, he had to scramble to move the four-poster bed away from the morning light that would shine in through the many skylights and rob him of energy and Ramona of what little life remained.

As the day brightened, his natural metabolism called to him to rest.

A shrill ring of the telephone woke him several hours later, but as it did, he became aware of the intense heat emanating from her body.

Her transformation had finally begun.

Chapter 24

Ignoring the phone call, he ran his hand across her forehead. Her skin burned beneath his palm, but her heart still beat as fast as a hummingbird's.

Maybe too weakly for her to survive.

Cradling her cheek, he passed his thumb across the flush of unnatural color there and called her name.

"Ramona. Wake, my love, and feed," he urged, hoping that yet another sampling of his blood would provide the needed fuel to keep her body going through the change.

In the background, the shrill ringing of the phone was followed by Ramona's voice on the answering machine. At the loud beep that followed, Diana's voice came across the line.

"Van Winter got a plea bargain deal negotiated already. Prosecutors were afraid his money could help him buy his way out of a prison term. They decided that ten years without parole in exchange for nailing John Henry for murder was a good outcome. I'm sorry," she said, and hung up.

Rage filled Diego and yet it didn't matter. He would exact his own punishment on the man if Ramona died. He might even do so if she survived, because justice had to be served.

Returning his attention to Ramona, he once again slashed open his arm, farther up now, since the skin on his wrists was too fragile for more punishment. He brought his forearm to her mouth and called her name again.

She barely opened her eyes, but it was enough to see the telltale glint of the vampire. At the smell of his blood, her eyes popped open and she latched on to his arm greedily, sucking and pulling.

With each tug his own demon responded, yearning to feed. Eager to sink into the soft flesh of her neck and the sweet, slick center of her. He fought it back, knowing there would be time enough if she survived the turning.

After a few minutes, she dropped back onto the bed, seemingly sated, until her body jerked upward and she cried out his name.

He straddled her and pinned her to the bed with his arms as she began to convulse, her body reacting to the vampire wanting dominion. Her breath rattled in her chest and she moaned, clearly in some misery. Wanting to ease that suffering, he dropped down onto her, gently trying to keep her from hurting herself.

Eventually she quieted and lay beneath him, drenched in sweat that evaporated quickly from the intense heat of her body. The earlier runaway beat of her heart became more languid, and with that came deeper and steadier breaths, until she seemed to be almost at rest.

Diego relaxed in turn, his vamp physiology reminding him that it was almost noon and not time for him to be up and about. His eyes had no sooner closed, however, when Ramona grew restless again.

Her body shook and trembled beneath him, slightly stronger than before. Taking that as a good sign, he fed her again, and now, for the first time, she drank deeply and well. When she sagged back onto the bed, her eyes were clear and glowing with the nearly reflective glare of the demon. At her incisors, he noticed the barest bump of fang.

"How do you feel?" he asked. Caressing her cheek, he lowered his thumb and ran it over her lips and that hint of fang.

"Weird. Warm. Hungry," she said, and her gaze drifted to his neck.

His own blood grew thick, pulsed heavily through his body and groin as he imagined her feeding on him. Imagined feeding on her and taking her at the same time. He shook his head to drive those thoughts away, and slowly slipped back into human form, wanting…no, needing that whatever happened next would be between man and woman.

As if understanding his cue, Ramona recaptured her human self, her eyes going back to their vibrant brown, though the trace of fang remained. With time she would learn to control it.

He finally believed there might actually be more days for them to spend together.

"Rest, *amor*. The fever will come again and you will need to feed once more."

Fear and sorrow colored his words, so powerfully that even in her dazed and altered state, Ramona recognized it. "I don't regret this."

A sad smile swept across his features. His human features. "May you feel the same way one hundred years from now."

One hundred years, she thought, and realized suddenly that she had no clue about his life. Where he had come from or how long he had been alive…or rather, undead.

"Tell me about yourself," she said, snuggling against his side. She listened as he told her his story, how he had been a callous and selfish lord who had lost his life and all his physical belongings, but gained something much more valuable—his honor and Esperanza.

Ramona's heart twisted at the other woman's name, recalling Diego's grief when she had passed. "You loved her a great deal."

Diego stroked Ramona's shoulder. "I did, only…this changed her."

"This? You mean, being a vampire?"

"She lost so much. Her life. Her family. All that we knew."

"You fear the same will happen to us. There is an 'us,' *sabes,*" she said, cupping his face in her hands and running her thumbs along his cheeks.

He smiled again and nodded. "There is. Now rest. We have a lifetime to talk."

And to love, she thought, closing her eyes and sinking against the hard warmth of his chest. Her body felt stronger, her heart light with the promise of life and the love of the man cradling her in his arms.

When the fever came again hours later, she knew there was no turning back. No return to her human life. And she didn't care.

Diego bared his neck to her, and at the sight, an inferno filled the center of her and exploded outward. Her head felt as if it might burst, but then there came a sudden release as her fangs erupted, nipping her lower lip as they elongated.

Saliva drenched her mouth and she imagined the taste of his skin. Of his blood.

He lowered his head and whispered against her lips, "Bite me."

She needed no further invitation.

The flesh of his neck gave way beneath the sharpness of her fangs. As she sucked, her head felt giddy and between her legs came a low, delicious throbbing that grew in intensity with each pull against the pulse in his neck.

Suddenly his hand was at her breast, working the tip into a hard peak until she wanted the satisfaction of his body more than she wanted his blood.

"Diego, love me," she cried, and he covered her mouth with his, licking away the remnants of his blood, sliding his tongue into her mouth. She tasted him, sweet and salty. His tongue mimicked the thrust of his body that was to come.

She pressed upward with her hips, and after a rush of hands and fingers, they were both naked, her hospital gown and his clothes tossed negligently onto the floor. She wanted him to rush then and take her, to drive into her over and over until release screamed through her. Instead he tarried, straddling her body and caressing her breasts, sucking each nipple into his mouth until she was begging for more. Even then he delayed, trailing his mouth down the center of her body, dropping kisses as he went until he reached her navel. He lingered there, tonguing the dainty indentation and eliciting a moan from her.

"That's it, *querida*. Enjoy this. Release yourself. Give me the woman to savor," he said, and with his words, a change came over her. A freedom to be anything and everything she had ever dreamed of being—and never dared to.

Applying pressure on his shoulders, she rolled him onto his back, bent and tongued his hard nipples. She loved the little delighted groan he gave and the way his erection pulsed against the tender flesh of her inner thigh.

When their gazes met, she realized he had reverted to his human self, as had she—when she ran her tongue along her upper teeth, there was no hint of a fang.

So this was how it would be, she thought, and didn't hesitate, wanting him no matter what he might be. She loved the heart inside the physical shell more than anything else.

She bent toward him, the tips of her breasts brushing the hard wall of his chest. She kissed him, and as she did so, reached down and encircled his erection. With slow, tender strokes, she built his passion, loving the bow of his body and the elegant line of his neck as he bent his head back, battling his release.

"It's okay, Diego. Show me your true self."

He groaned and looked at her, his eyes glowing, the hint of fang visible below his lip. "Love me," he pleaded.

She guided him to her center and positioned him at the entrance of her womb. As she slowly accepted him into her body, she said, "I do, Diego. I do love you."

Diego grasped her hips as she moved on him, urging her on as she rode him. He reined in his need, because when he finally released it, the vampire would want its due.

She tired above him and he rolled over,

bringing her beneath him. He increased the strength of his thrusts and she answered, gripping his shoulders and urging him on, lifting her knees and wrapping her legs around his waist to deepen his penetration.

He needed more and sought her breast, sucking on the sweet tip. Desiring another kind of satisfaction, he carefully lowered his fangs, ran the sharp tip along the hard point of her nipple. She shuddered and her heartbeat picked up in speed.

Meeting her gaze, his breath rasping in his throat, he said, "I want a taste."

Her eyes bled out to the eerie green of the demon, and from beneath her upper lip, her fangs glided down. "I'm ready," she said, but he knew she wasn't. She had yet to experience even a small part of the pleasure to be had. He intended to show her.

He plunged deep into her center and didn't withdraw, wanting to be tight in her body's embrace during the passion he was about to unleash.

He sucked on her beaded nipple, grazed it once again with his teeth before gently sinking them into the tender flesh.

She called out his name and muscles clenched on his erection, milking him closer and closer to satisfaction.

He dammed the flood of emotion, wanting her more than he had ever wanted anyone else. Wanting to please her more than he wanted life itself. As he released his bite, he licked the small nicks left by his fangs, healing them with his tongue.

Then he moved in her again, one hand braced on the bed, the other caressing her breast until she arched her hips upward, asking for more.

He made her beg. Then, with a slow, nearly maddening descent, he filled her until Ramona was writhing beneath him. Tremors racked her body and his. He could hear the strong, insistent beat of her heart, almost calling out to him.

Love me. Love me. Love me.

And he did.

He bent his head and nuzzled her face, shifting aside her long chestnut locks to reveal the crook of her neck.

She did the same, brushing aside his hair and positioning her mouth by his jugular. She traced the skin there with the sharp points of her teeth.

At that, he finally lost control, sank his teeth into her, and she did the same.

The sensation of her putting the bite on him opened an emotional and physical floodgate. His body shook as he took his satisfaction, driving deep into her, no longer fearful of hurting her, because she was no longer a fragile human.

She murmured something unintelligible, but dug her nails into his shoulder, letting him know it was all about passion now and not pain.

He fed until his body climaxed, pouring his undead seed into her core. She gave one last pull with her mouth and then released him, crying out. She called his name and cradled his head to her, raining kiss after kiss against his face.

As they dropped down together onto the mattress, Diego fit her into his side, unwilling to let go of her. She nestled close, clearly not wanting to leave him, either.

When they regained control and their human forms reigned once more, Ramona teased, "Tell me about yourself...again."

"It's a long long story." He laid a hand at her waist and pulled her tight, but she sat up, a playful smile on her face and life shining from her dark brown eyes.

"We have all the time in the world," she said, and kissed him.

As he returned the kiss, he realized how strong and determined she had been even in the face of death. How her passion for life and for him transcended mortal bounds, and would feed their souls for all eternity. He knew then that Ramona was right.

They had all the time in the world to be together.

* * * * *

Look for the next book in THE CALLING.
Coming soon from Caridad Piñeiro
and Silhouette Nocturne.

Mediterranean Nights

Join the guests and crew of Alexandra's Dream, *the newest luxury ship to set sail on the romantic Mediterranean, as they experience the glamorous world of cruising.*

A new Harlequin continuity series begins in June 2007 with FROM RUSSIA, WITH LOVE by Ingrid Weaver.

Marina Artamova books a cabin on the luxurious cruise ship Alexandra's Dream, *when she finds out that her orphaned nephew and his adoptive father are aboard. She's determined to be reunited with the boy...but the romantic ambience of the ship and her undeniable attraction to a man she considers her enemy are about to interfere with her quest!*

Turn the page for a sneak preview!

Piraeus, Greece

"THERE SHE IS, Stefan. *Alexandra's Dream*." David Anderson squatted beside his new son and pointed at the dark blue hull that towered above the pier. The cruise ship was a majestic sight, twelve decks high and as long as a city block. A circle of silver and gold stars, the logo of the Liberty Cruise Line, gleamed from the swept-back smokestack. Like some legendary sea creature born for the water, the ship emanated power from every sleek curve—even at rest it held the promise of motion. "That's going to be our home for the next ten days."

The child beside him remained silent, his cheeks working in and out as he sucked furiously on his thumb. Hair so blond it appeared white ruffled against his forehead in the harbor breeze. The baby-sweet scent unique to the very young mingled with the tang of the sea.

"Ship," David said. "Uh, *parakhod*."

From beneath his bangs, Stefan looked at the

Alexandra's Dream. Although he didn't release his thumb, the corners of his mouth tightened with the beginning of a smile.

David grinned. That was Stefan's first smile this afternoon, one of only two since they had left the orphanage yesterday. It was probably because of the boat—according to the orphanage staff, the boy loved boats, which was the main reason David had decided to book this cruise. Then again, there was a strong possibility the smile could have been a reaction to David's attempt at pocket-dictionary Russian. Whatever the cause, it was a good start.

The liaison from the adoption agency had claimed that Stefan had been taught some English, but David had yet to see evidence of it. David continued to speak, positive his son would understand his tone even if he couldn't grasp the words. "This is her maiden voyage. Her first trip, just like this is our first trip, and that makes it special." He motioned toward the stage that had been set up on the pier beneath the ship's bow. "That's why everyone's celebrating."

The ship's official christening ceremony had been held the day before and had been a closed affair, with only the cruise-line executives and VIP guests invited, but the stage hadn't yet been disassembled. Banners bearing the blue and white of the Greek flag of the ship's owner, as well as the Liberty circle of stars logo, draped the edges of the platform. In the center, a group of musicians and a dance troupe dressed in traditional white folk costumes performed for the benefit of the *Alexandra's Dream*'s first passengers. Their audience was in a festive mood, snapping their fingers in time to the music while the dancers twirled and wove through their steps.

David bobbed his head to the rhythm of the mandolins. They were playing a folk tune that seemed vaguely familiar, possibly from a movie he'd seen. He hummed a few notes. "Catchy melody, isn't it?"

Stefan turned his gaze on David. His eyes were a striking shade of blue, as cool and pale as a winter horizon and far too solemn for a child not yet five. Still, the smile that hovered at the corners of his mouth persisted. He moved his head with the music, mirroring David's motion.

David gave a silent cheer at the interaction. Hopefully, this cruise would provide countless opportunities for more. "Hey, good for you," he said. "Do you like the music?"

The child's eyes sparked. He withdrew his thumb with a pop. *"Moozika!"*

"Music. Right!" David held out his hand. "Come on, let's go closer so we can watch the dancers."

Stefan grasped David's hand quickly, as if he feared it would be withdrawn. In an instant his budding smile was replaced by a look close to panic.

Did he remember the car accident that had killed his parents? It would be a mercy if he didn't. As far as David knew, Stefan had never spoken of it to anyone. Whatever he had seen had made him run so far from the crash that the police hadn't found him until the next day. The event had traumatized him to the extent that he hadn't uttered a word until his fifth week at the orphanage. Even now he seldom talked.

David sat back on his heels and brushed the hair from Stefan's forehead. That solemn, too-old gaze locked with his, and for an instant, David felt as if he looked back in time at an image of himself thirty years ago.

He didn't need to speak the same language to understand exactly how this boy felt. He knew what it meant to be alone and powerless among strangers, trying to be brave and tough but wishing with every fiber of his being for a place to belong, to be safe, and most of all for someone to love him....

He knew in his heart he would be a good parent to Stefan. It was why he had never considered halting the adoption process after Ellie had left him. He hadn't balked when he'd learned of the recent claim by Stefan's spinster aunt, either; the absentee relative had shown up too late for her case to be considered. The adoption was meant to be. He and this child already shared a bond that went deeper than paperwork or legalities.

A seagull screeched overhead, making Stefan start and press closer to David.

"That's my boy," David murmured. He swallowed hard, struck by the simple truth of what he had just said.

That's my *boy.*

"I CAN'T BE PATIENT, RUDOLPH. I'm not going to stand by and watch my nephew get ripped from his country and his roots to live on the other side of the world."

Rudolph hissed out a slow breath. "Marina, I don't like the sound of that. What are you planning?"

"I'm going to talk some sense into this American kidnapper."

"No. Absolutely not. No offence, but diplomacy is not your strong suit."

"Diplomacy be damned. Their ship's due to sail at five o'clock."

"Then you wouldn't have an opportunity to speak with him even if his lawyer agreed to a meeting."

"I'll have ten days of opportunities, Rudolph, since I plan to be on board that ship."

* * * * *

Follow Marina and David as they join forces to uncover the reason behind little Stefan's unusual silence, and the secret behind the death of his parents....

Look for From Russia, With Love *by Ingrid Weaver in stores June 2007.*

Silhouette

nocturne™

COMING NEXT MONTH

#17 RAINTREE: HAUNTED • Linda Winstead Jones
The Raintree Trilogy (Book 2 of 3)
Born with the ability to speak to earthbound spirits, Gideon Raintree made a startlingly good homicide detective. But when his newly assigned partner, Hope Malory, arrived in Wilmington, she saw Gideon as a mystery waiting to be unraveled—and was given her chance when the Ansara wizards came to hunt the forgotten son of the Raintree clan.

#18 UNBOUND • Lori Devoti
Risk Leidolf was a hellhound—a legendary creature who could take either human or canine form—and he was in bondage to a malevolent witch. But when the evil witch asked him to hunt down innocent Kara Shane and destroy her, the man within him rebelled. Risk quickly devised a plan that with success would break him free—but if it failed, he'd lose his humanity and the only woman he could ever love.

SNCNM0507